BLAKE MICHAEL NELSON

This one's for Zach and Mattea

CHAPTER ONE

*K*aden had been in a *lot* of fights. He'd had his jaw broken, his eyes blackened, and his face bloodied dozens of times; he'd taken hits to the midsection that had doubled him over, dropping him to his knees, making him retch; and his arms and hands had been slashed open so often—by swords, spears, and knives—that you could almost play tic-tac-toe over the crisscrossing scars.

He'd been in a lot of fights. He *liked* to fight; he liked the excitement, the challenge. He liked putting his skills to the test.

Alas, the only thing being tested tonight was his patience.

He sighed.

The first guy was a big, grunting brute, with hairy arms and a massive chest. He had a bit of a gut, though, and he moved like molasses; Kaden didn't have any trouble avoiding his clumsy attempt to tackle him. As the man changed direction, grabbing for him, Kaden gave him a quick slap across the face with one of his tonfa—just to wake him up—and then struck him in the chest with a perfectly-executed jump-kick. The brute's sheer meatiness absorbed some of the impact, but it was a good, solid kick, and more than enough to knock him down. He fell to the pavement, gasping.

The second guy was a bit trickier. For starters, he had a knife—a long, fixed-blade knife, with a blade so shiny that it caught the light of the street lamps. It was a wicked-looking thing.

The man was also much warier than the brute; he obviously

wasn't the kind to rush in without thinking. He began circling Kaden, studying him with crafty eyes, all the while holding the knife extended out in front of him like a talisman. He probably expected him to be intimidated by the ugly blade, but Kaden wasn't even looking at the knife—he was looking at how the man was holding it. Crafty's grip was all wrong—it was too loose—and he was holding it too far away from his body. Kaden wondered if he'd ever actually used the thing. Probably not; probably the sight of it alone was enough to frighten most people. That was why he was holding it like a talisman, rather than a weapon.

The man was waiting for him to make the first move, so Kaden obliged, feinting a few times before rushing in. Crafty's response was predictable—he started doing the stabby-stabby thing that people with knives do when someone starts crowding them. Kaden caught a couple of the stabby-stabs with his tonfa, just for fun, then ended the flurry by casually swatting the big knife out of the creep's hand with one tonfa and giving him a hard crack on the skull with the other. Crafty went down, and stayed down.

Easy. Kaden sighed again.

By now the brute had recovered his wits, but he was clearly done fighting. He sat there on the pavement, morose. "Damn," he muttered, more to himself than to Kaden.

Further down the street, about thirty feet away, Quentin was having his own fun: he was battling the group's ringleader, the Rhythm, a clever bare-knuckle fighter. The Rhythm was a good martial artist, with an unpredictable style; he fought to the beat of the music he listened to (his headphones seemed to have been bolted on to his head). His unpredictable kicks and punches threw some fighters off, but Quentin wasn't having any trouble with him. Blocking the man's fists with his whirling staff, he pressed in close, ducking and dodging...and then, in the midst of this whirlwind, he somehow pivoted *around* the man, pummeling him with short blows, one after the other, before finally sweeping him off his feet and pinning him to the asphalt with the butt of his staff. Kaden had seen Quentin pull this pivoting-around trick several times before, but he'd never been able to emulate it. Quentin was *really* good with that *bō*.

Well, that was why they called him Quarterstaff.

Kaden dragged his two hoodlums over to Quentin, who added the Rhythm to the pile. "Nice work," the blond-headed hero told his sidekick. "They give you any trouble?"

"*These* guys? Are you kidding me?"

Quentin shrugged. "Sometimes they surprise you."

He snorted derisively, glancing down at the sorry-looking pile of crooks. "I'm sure. What happened to that thing they stole?"

"The Rhythm dropped it back in that alley where we jumped them. Go fetch it, would you?"

"Right." Dropping his tonfa into the sheaths on his thighs, he jogged out of the street and turned into the damp, dark alley where he and Quarterstaff had launched their attack on the thieves. The stolen merchandise, taken from a Kite Laboratories facility less than an hour ago, was lying in the middle of the alley; Kaden walked over to it.

It was a black, hard-plastic cylinder, about the size and shape of a golf bag, with a black handle in the center and a lid and a latch on one end. A couple of bright-yellow warning stickers had been applied to it, but Kaden couldn't make out what was written on them; it was too dark.

It was obviously some kind of carrying case. But what was inside it, and why had the Rhythm and his hired thugs gone to so much trouble to steal it? He frowned at the object for a second or two, then reached down to pick it up.

He paused, though, just as he was about to wrap his fingers around the handle. Something had caught his eye—a bit of movement to his left, a shifting of the shadows in the darkest part of the alley. He frowned again. What was...?

And then, without warning, a dark figure suddenly burst out of the shadows and kicked him right in the face.

It wasn't a knockout blow—there wasn't much force behind it—but it stung, and it surprised the hell out of him.

Jerking upright, he found himself face to face—or mask to mask, anyway—with a shadowy figure, dressed all in black (but for a pair of white sneakers), who was just then getting ready to spin-kick him a second time. Fortunately, he saw this one coming; the white of the sneakers was easy to follow in the half-light. Blocking the cartwheeling kick with his left forearm, he stepped inside to deliver a punch with his right hand.

It was a sloppy counter, though, and it was slow; he was still a little stunned from that kick to the face. The shadowy figure, lightning-fast, ducked under the punch, slipped under his extended arm, and hammered an elbow into his side. Like the kick, there wasn't a lot of power behind the blow, but it hit him in just the right spot, between the plates of his body armor, and it made him wince. He took a step back.

Apparently satisfied, the shadow flitted away from him, grabbed the cylinder, and made a break for it down the alley. Snarling, Kaden immediately gave chase, but the shadow was a lithe, speedy little thing, and a fast runner in those sneakers.

How in the world had the little ninja managed to get so close, without his noticing?

He followed his attacker out of the alley, and onto a darkened street. The ninja was outpacing him, though, and after ducking into another chiaroscuro alley the shadowy little sucker-puncher simply vanished, swallowed up by the darkness.

Kaden swore. Giving the dark alley a final, parting look, he gave a nearby wall a frustrated slap and made his way back to Quentin.

"What happened?" the hero asked, when he returned.

He scowled. "I got jumped."

"Oh?"

"There was someone hiding in the shadows. Whoever he was, he made off with the merchandise."

"They must've had another accomplice." He looked down at the thieves. Crafty was still unconscious, and the Rhythm never, ever spoke (the rumor was he'd suffered some kind of brain damage as a child), so Quentin fixed his attention on the big, hairy-armed guy. "All right, princess," he said, prodding the man with the butt of his staff. "Start talking. What'd you steal and why'd you steal it?"

"I don't know what it was," the man said. "Honest. I was just along for the ride."

"Who hired you?"

The man glanced at the Rhythm, whose face was impassive. "He did."

"And who hired *him*? The Rhythm wasn't behind that heist; there's no way he figured that one out himself. Who's he working for?"

"I don't know. I don't know anything about that."

"Okay. What about the guy in the alley, who jumped my partner just now? Know anything about him?" He gave him another prod

4

with his staff.

He shook his head vigorously. "No, no. I don't know anything."

"He's lying," Kaden said.

Quentin sighed. "No. I don't think so. This guy's just a subcontractor; I don't think the Rhythm gave him a hell of a lot of info."

The police arrived a few minutes later to take the goons into custody. Kaden and Quentin, watching the cops do their work from the roof of a nearby building, proceeded to speculate.

"So who do *you* think hired the Rhythm?" Kaden asked.

"Not sure," he said, tugging thoughtfully at his goatee. "All I know is it wasn't the Rhythm who planned that one out. The doors were unlocked remotely, and the security cameras were fried. Slick job. Someone was helping them."

"*I've* got a suspect," Kaden ventured.

"Oh? Do tell."

"I think it was the Dark."

Quentin considered that, resting his chin on the end of his staff. "Okay. Let's hear your reasoning."

"The Rhythm's worked for the Dark before; they've hired him several times."

"Yeah, for grunt work, sure. This was a sophisticated heist, though; you really think they'd trust him to pull off something like this?" He shook his head. "I don't think—"

"That's not all. The one in the alley—the one who jumped me—was Academy-trained."

"Are you sure?"

Kaden gave the man a gimme-a-break kind of look. "I *know* the Academy style, Quentin. It's *my* style. I grew up with those people, remember?"

He frowned. "I remember. Isn't it possible this person you fought in the alley was just a former student, though, with no *current* connection to the Dark? The Matsumoto Academy has trained dozens and dozens of fighters over the years; not all of them have stayed with the syndicate."

Kaden ran a hand through his dark hair. "It's possible, but...I don't know. I have a funny feeling about this one."

Quentin nodded. "Okay. We'll look into it." He gave his sidekick a sidelong look. "Let's call it a night."

"It's early."

"You've got school tomorrow."

"So?"

"School's important."

"You dropped out of school when you were sixteen," the youth reminded him. "You were younger than I am now." Kaden had turned seventeen a few months ago.

"Everyone makes mistakes," Quentin said offhandedly, twirling his staff around in an absent sort of way. "And anyway, I could *afford* to screw up; my old man was one of the richest men in the country. Most people aren't quite so fortunate."

Kaden couldn't argue with *that*—very, very few people were as fortunate as Quentin Daniels. He was wealthy, handsome, tall, charming, a terrific athlete, and a skilled martial artist, who excelled in practically everything he did. He owned a gigantic company, the Daniels Corporation, and lived in a huge, luxury condominium on the fifty-sixth floor of a major downtown skyscraper, the Daniels Tower. His father had been rich; his grandfather had been rich (and a U.S. senator besides). Silver spoons.

Kaden hadn't had Quentin's luck. He'd been raised by his uncle, John Gargan, a rumpled informant for the secretive crime syndicate known as the Dark. His childhood had been a chaotic mess of trashy apartments, garbage takeout, spotty school attendance, and lonely, unhappy holidays (Christmas was the worst). And after Gargan had handed him over to the Matsumoto Academy—the martial arts school where the Dark's enforcers got their training—well, his life certainly hadn't gotten any easier at that point. The Academy's instructors were brutal.

His luck *had* finally begun to turn around a few years ago, after he left the Academy and met Quentin—probably some of the man's own luck had rubbed off on him—but his life was, overall, still pretty chaotic. Superheroes' lives tended to be.

Quentin twirled his staff around some more, as they turned away from the scene and began making their way home. He whistled as he walked; Quentin had always been a cheery guy. "You probably won't see too much of me tomorrow," he said. "I'm on call for Personal Support all afternoon, and I'll be going out with Diane in the evening."

"The supermodel?"

"Yeah."

"Hmph. Lucky you."

Quentin's response to that was a big, goofy grin, one that showed off his perfectly straight, perfectly white teeth. "We make our *own* luck, Kaden."

It was one of his favorite sayings.

CHAPTER TWO

Quentin had assumed guardianship of Kaden three years ago, shortly after the murder of his uncle. He lived in the Daniels Tower now, on a quiet floor situated just below Quentin's penthouse, and attended an elite private school—the Jeffries School, it was called—in Signal City's leafy, Victorian-style Stone's Row neighborhood, on the far northern tip of the peninsula. He hadn't done all that well on the entrance exam—they didn't teach trigonometry at the Matsumoto Academy—but Quentin had pulled some strings, and the (expensive) tutors he'd hired had eventually brought him up to speed.

Kaden's life at the Academy had been spartan, to say the least, and living in the Daniels Tower, where he had his own apartment—along with a maid, and a driver, and a full-time chef—had taken some getting used to. He *had* eventually gotten used to it, though.

School was different; he'd never really managed to adjust to school life. Spending whole days sitting at a *desk*, wearing a dumb uniform, listening to dweeby pencil-neck teachers dispense useless trivia, all the while surrounded by annoying trust-fund kids...well, it was a chore, and a bore, and he only really put up with it because Quentin insisted.

His fellow classmates were the sons and daughters of politicians, CEO's, and celebrities, and none of them quite knew what to make of Kaden. Wanting for nothing, leading lives of comfort and frivolity, vacationing in Saint-Tropez and taking selfies at every opportunity, they had a hard time relating to the brooding, serious Kaden, and he had a hard time relating to them. Needless to say, he didn't have any real friends at Jeffries...and he didn't particularly wanted any. What he *wanted* was to be left alone.

Unfortunately, the kid sitting across the table from him was stubbornly refusing to get the message.

"Hey! Is this true? It says here Batterypack is retiring!" The kid was studying the latest issue of *Champions Weekly*, while absently chowing down on a cheeseburger. "I didn't know anything about this. Did you know anything about this? How old is he, anyway?"

"I don't know, Race," Kaden sighed.

"He started out back in the '90's, right? No one's ever seen him without that helmet, so I guess no one really knows how old he is...but man! Batterypack! He's been around forever! It's not gonna be the same scene without him, you know?" He took another bite of his burger and turned the page of his magazine. "I wonder if he'll pass that suit of his on to someone else."

"I don't know, Race," he sighed (again). Race was the same age as Kaden, but it was hard not to think of him as a kid—he was a smiley, excitable type, with bright blue eyes that opened up hugely whenever they fell on anything remotely interesting. And he was small for his age, too, shorter even than Kaden (who only stood about five-seven...or five-eight, in his sneakers).

The kid was also *obsessed* with Signal City's superheroes. Following the superhero gossip was a pretty common pastime, of course, but Race took it to a ridiculous level: he was a complete fanboy, who kept copies of *Aces* and *Sixgun's Metahuman Review* in his backpack and who could probably rattle off the names, and special abilities, of every hero and villain in the city.

Kaden wondered how the kid would react if he found out *he* was moonlighting as a superhero. Would his head explode? It seemed like a distinct possibility.

"Oh, this is bad," Race continued, a bit of chewed-up burger flying out of his mouth. "You remember Hypnotika? She escaped from the Metahuman Correctional Center about six months ago."

"Yes, yes, I remember."

"Someone spotted her in Stone's Row the other day. Huh! I wonder what she's up to. And listen to this: the Quantum Man is planning on installing a polythetic dampener on the new Barathrum

Bridge." He swallowed the remainder of his burger. "I wonder when they're gonna get around to rebuilding that thing. They put my dad on the committee, you know; he says they haven't even seen the proposals yet. Oh! And did you hear what happened to Nailgun? He knocked over that armored car last week..."

And so it went. Every lunch period was the same; Kaden would find an empty table in the dining hall, sit down, and begin eating his lunch...and then, inevitably, Race would show up, uninvited, and start yammering at him about superhero stuff. The kid was friendly, and harmless, but he could get to be pretty annoying. Kaden had no idea why he'd latched on to him.

Race was just wrapping up some story about one of his favorite heroes, the brawler Brazen, when some kind of disturbance suddenly broke out on the other side of the dining hall. Race's blue eyes opened hugely. "What's going on over there?" he wondered.

The sudden outburst had quieted down the cafeteria. Kaden, not really all that interested, nevertheless leaned back a bit in his seat to get a better look.

He recognized the participants from his history class. Angel Middleford, an unpleasant, overweight girl with a pierced eyebrow and a deep, bellowing voice (it had been *her* shouting that had cut across the cafeteria) was yelling something or other at another girl, a pretty blonde, who was sitting calmly in her seat. When the blonde replied to Angel, in a voice too quiet for Kaden to hear, the chubby girl responded with "I know what you meant!" and proceeded to throw an apple at her. It missed.

Finally, noticing the crowd, the irate Angel turned up her nose, sniffed, and exited the cafeteria with a couple of her hangers-on. She always seemed to have a couple of hangers-on.

The blonde girl, meanwhile, returned to her meal, her expression blank.

"Angel," Race muttered, as the cafeteria noise returned to normal. "Figures. Who was she yelling at? I couldn't see."

"Izzy," Kaden replied absently.

"Izzy..."

"Izzy Rushforth."

"Oh! Okay, I know who you're talking about. Isidora Rushforth. Transferred here at the beginning of the year, right? Do you know her?"

"Only her name. She sits next to me in history."

"I heard she was kind of stuck-up."

"I wouldn't know. I've never spoken with her."

"The Rushforths have a *lot* of money," Race commented thoughtfully. "I guess it wouldn't surprise me, to learn she was stuck-up."

"*Everyone* here comes from money," Kaden pointed out.

"Yeah, but the Rushforths are in a whole 'nother league. I wonder why she even transferred here?"

"I don't know, Race," he sighed (yet again). He got up to leave; he'd just finished his own burger and he was, by now, starting to get a little tired of Race's nonstop prattle. "Catch ya later."

He passed the blonde girl, Izzy, on his way out. She was still there, still eating her lunch.

No one else was sitting at her table.

* * *

He was just leaving school, later that same day, when he got a call from Quentin. "I've got some news," he said.

"Good or bad?"

"Kind of a mix. Here's the good: I managed to find out what it was that the Rhythm stole from Kite Laboratories last night."

"Oh? What was it?"

"A bunch of swords."

"Swords?"

"Yeah, three swords, to be exact—Externian *ji'dar* blades, forged about seven thousand years ago by some Externian sorcerer. They look similar to Japanese katanas, but they're made out of some unusual metal, and apparently they've got some really strange, really unique properties."

"Magic?"

"Sounded like it."

"So what were they doing at Kite Labs?"

"They were being studied. The Paranormals brought them back from Externia the last time they visited the place; Kite was borrowing them."

Kaden absorbed that. "Stolen swords, huh? You know what I'm thinking?"

"Yeah. It's looking more and more like the Dark was behind this one. And this might not have been the *only* one."

"What do you mean?"

"There've been other thefts. Someone stole a pair of enchanted *kama* from a local collector about a month ago, and just last week a couple of Epee's diuturnal blades were stolen from Armitage's auction house before they could be sold. There may have been other robberies, too; these are just the ones I know about."

"So the Dark is going around stealing magical weaponry."

"Well, not all of these weapons are necessarily magical; some are just strange, or have strange properties, like Epee's old swords." He paused. "And there's one more wrinkle."

"I'm listening."

"The police detective who was investigating these thefts—a guy named Joe Arroyo—was murdered in his apartment last night. He was stabbed."

"One of the Dark's assassins, no doubt," Kaden said. "Yeng, maybe, or Edge, or one of the Gao twins. So what's our next step?"

"I'd like you to check out Arroyo's apartment tonight. The Dark obviously had him killed for a reason; maybe he had some idea of what they were up to."

"I can do that, sure...but wait, you won't be joining me?"

"Sorry. I'm flying to the U.K. in a couple of hours...and I probably won't be back until November."

Kaden started. "What? Why? I thought you had a date with Diane tonight."

"Change of plans. I'm going to be helping Garnet train for the Grail Quest." Garnet, Kaden recalled, was one of the U.K.'s premier superheroes. "He burned his powers out fighting Tannakin Skinker last year, and now he has to go through this whole quest thing to get them back. It's a lot of preparation."

"So you'll be overseas for the next two months."

"Just about. And unfortunately Garnet is something of a Luddite, so I may be without my cell phone for a while. You'll be flying solo."

Kaden raised an eyebrow. "You're trusting me to handle this investigation all by myself? This is new."

"I think you're ready. You're a better fighter than I was at your age, and savvier." He paused for a moment, then added, "Besides,

I'm not getting any younger, kid. I'll be thirty-six next year, and thirty-six is old for this business, especially when you play the game like I've been playing it. The guys like us...the guys without powers...we don't have long careers."

"Ah."

"So, bottom line, I need Skirmish to start getting some real experience out there, before...well, before I retire."

Kaden knew what this meant. Quentin had had several reasons for taking him under his wing, but it had been obvious from the start that he'd been grooming him to be his successor.

He frowned at the thought. It wasn't as though Quentin was *forcing* him into anything—he'd *wanted* to become the man's sidekick —but he *did* have some reservations about striking out on his own. He liked going out at night, and he liked the fighting, but...

Well, that was the problem: the fighting.

For now, though, he simply nodded along; this wasn't something he felt like discussing over the phone. "I get it. I'll check out Arroyo's apartment tonight. I'll let you know what I find...if I can get ahold of you. Have a nice trip."

"Thanks, kid. Stay safe." And he hung up.

Kaden put the phone in his pocket and stepped outside. It was a nice afternoon; the sky was a deep, dark blue, and the cherry blossom trees, which dotted the school grounds, had just turned a lovely shade of autumn red. Kaden slung his backpack over his shoulder, gave the scene a brief, contemplative look, and headed for the parking lot. Most of the kids at Jeffries had their drivers pick them up, but Kaden preferred to drive himself to school.

Leaving the grounds through the front gate, he hit the sidewalk and began making his way east. The parking lot was behind the main building, which made for a rather long and tedious walk, but it was such a nice day that he didn't mind.

He was just passing through a little landscaped area when he suddenly heard a voice—a deep, bellowing voice—coming out of a copse of trees, about thirty feet to his right. Curious, he threw a glance in that direction.

The voice, he was not surprised to learn, belonged to Angel Middleford. She, and a couple of her hangers-on, were looming, rather menacingly, over Izzy Rushforth, who was seated on a bench that had been placed beneath the cherry trees. She had a book in her hands, and the same neutral expression on her face that Kaden had seen her wearing at lunch.

More of this, he mused, stopping to watch.

"What're you reading?" Angel asked, a second before snatching the book away. "What is this? Poetry?" She tossed the book away in disgust. "You're such a poseur." She took a step forward, leaning over her even more menacingly. "You really think you're better than me, don't you?"

The blonde looked up at her. "Yes, actually."

One of Angel's followers—Mallory was her name—responded to *that* by picking up Izzy's backpack, which she had sitting beside her on the bench, and dumping the contents out on the grass. Books, papers, and pencils flew out.

"You're pissing me off," Angel growled. "You must not be very smart." She bent down to face her. "So here, I'll make it plain: I'm gonna make your life *miserable* for the next eight months. I don't care who your daddy is, you stupid little poseur; someone gets on my bad side, they pay the price." She reached into her purse and pulled out a chocolate pudding cup. "And just so you don't forget..."

And she proceeded to dump the pudding on Izzy's head. The other girls laughed, making scatological comments.

"See you around," Angel said, throwing the empty pudding cup at her as a parting shot. It bounced off her shoulder.

Izzy sat there for a long moment, with the chocolate pudding on her blonde head and her belongings scattered all over. She really *was* quite pretty, Kaden thought, even in this disheveled state; her features were soft and delicate, her skin fair, her eyes a pale, icy blue. Her platinum-blonde hair was long and straight, falling past her shoulders, framing her face. She was a real head-turner.

Kaden, being a guy, had naturally thrown a glance or two her way during the boring history class they shared...but she was so reserved, so quiet, so aloof, that he'd never bothered to try to get to know her. And he doubted anyone else at Jeffries had, either.

Another moment passed, and Izzy, at last, got up off the bench and began collecting her things. Her expression was still blank; had Angel's threats and bullying made any impression on her at all? It didn't look like it.

She was reaching down to pick up her poetry book when she spotted Kaden, who was still standing on the sidewalk, watching her.

Their eyes met.

Kaden saw *something* in those eyes—defiance, maybe?—but he didn't hold her gaze for long; he turned away as soon as she spotted him, adjusting his backpack on his shoulder and hurrying on his way. It was an...awkward moment.

He shook his head, angry at himself. What was *wrong* with him? Why didn't...why didn't he...?

You can run away from us, a voice reminded him. *But you can't run away from yourself.*

Kaden scowled. He hated that voice.

CHAPTER THREE

*H*e made it back to the Daniels Tower around five o'clock. Kaden had a floor all to himself—it was a sleek, modern suite, with a full kitchen, a dining room, and even a balcony (which offered a terrific view of the city)—but he'd never really bothered to furnish it; most of the suite was just an open, empty expanse of gray carpet and glossy wood flooring. He had a couch, a TV, a desk, and some exercise equipment, and that was really all he needed.

After eating a quick, microwaved dinner, he watched the news, did some homework, and, after the sun went down, suited up. He kept his equipment in a big, locked chest, made of heavy plastic, which he kept in his closet.

There wasn't much to his outfit—lightweight, shiny-black body armor, boots, gloves, and a belt with a few tools and gadgets, most of which he never used. A strip of black cloth, with a couple of holes cut out for his eyes, served as a mask; he tied this around his head, *hachimaki*-style. The black matched his eyes, and hair.

His weapons were fairly simple, too: a pair of black tonfa, a knife, and a collapsible, concealable dart gun that Quentin had given him. The gun was a heavy, high-tech thing, designed by some egghead scientist at the Daniels Corporation, and it came with a whole assortment of specialized darts—one kind of dart had an exploding tip, and another contained a tranquilizer—but Kaden had never found much use for the thing; his specialty was close-quarters combat. He only carried it in case he had to blow something up.

He took the private elevator down to the parking garage, retrieved his motorcycle from the secret room Quentin had installed, and headed for Joe Arroyo's apartment. According to the information Quentin had texted him, Arroyo had lived in a nine-story building just south of Stone's Row, on the edge of downtown. It wasn't a very nice neighborhood.

He parked his motorcycle in an alley across the street and gave the building a long look. Like most of the apartment complexes in the neighborhood, it was a rather plain-looking brick building, probably built in the 1950's, with air conditioners jutting out of just about every window and jangly fire-escape stairways running all along its western side.

Arroyo's apartment was on the top floor. It was likely still a crime scene, and going in through the front door didn't seem like a particularly good idea, so Kaden decided to make use of those fire escapes: he crossed the street, ducked into the adjoining alley, and began acrobatting his way up to the top floor. Fortunately the fire escapes weren't quite as jangly as they looked; they held firm and didn't make too much noise as he climbed them.

The door at the top was, of course, locked. Looking around, he spotted a likely window and hopped off the fire escape, tiptoeing along the edge of the building's protruding brickwork in order to reach it. The window, as it turned out, was also locked, but Kaden's knife made short work of the locking mechanism. Sliding it open, and pushing the shade out of the way, he gave the interior a quick check —the window appeared to lead into a kitchen—and clambered inside.

The apartment was dark, and appeared to be unoccupied. Removing a small LED flashlight from his belt, he clicked it on, and almost immediately spotted the residue of a nasty-looking bloodstain on the tiled kitchen floor. Someone had mopped up the worst of it, but the blood had soaked into a rug, and there was splatter all over a nearby wall. Little yellow evidence tags had been placed all over the scene.

Clearly he was in the right place.

Kaden didn't think he'd get much out of the murder scene itself, and so exited the kitchen, moving into a living room. The place was actually pretty nice; it was small, but tidy, and very well-appointed.

Framed, family photographs had been hung all over the living room walls, and pictures of happy, smiling children decorated the man's computer desk. These were probably nieces or nephews or something; the detective himself had been a lifelong bachelor, and, according to Quentin, had never had any kids.

Kaden had been hoping to get a look at the man's computer, but the police had evidently confiscated it; there was nothing on the desk now but a couple of detached cables. There *were* some folders in the detective's desk, but after leafing through the papers inside, Kaden decided he wasn't going to find anything relevant in them and put them back where he'd found them.

There was a wastepaper basket next to the computer desk. Kaden knew from experience that interesting things could sometimes be found in wastepaper baskets—Quentin had cracked the Rolfe case, for example, by finding a pay slip from Thinktwice in the man's garbage—and decided that it might be worth checking out. He pulled several pieces of crumpled-up paper out of the basket and flattened them out on the desk.

Most of the papers were uninteresting, but one caught his eye— a hastily-scribbled note that read, "Check witness account, Lopez case, possible link to Armitage robbery." The Armitage robbery, he remembered, was one of the heists Quentin had mentioned. Kaden didn't know what this "Lopez case" was all about, or what the connection might be, but it seemed like a clue, so he stuffed the scrap of paper in a pocket and resolved to look into it.

There didn't seem to be anything else of interest in the apartment. Kaden, satisfied with what he'd collected, returned to the kitchen window, pausing for a moment to take in the crime scene. Which one of the Dark's assassins had murdered the detective? It was too messy to have been Yeng's work, and not messy enough to have been the work of the Gao twins. Edge, maybe? The Blades? He supposed it could've been any one of them.

Stepping around the evidence tags, he pushed the shade aside a second time and slid back out the window. He was just regaining his footing on the fire escape when a voice, a female voice, suddenly called out to him. "Who are you?"

He looked up...

...And started at what he saw.

It was a young woman, hooded, wearing a huge, fluttering white cloak. The cloak was one of the strangest, most astonishing things Kaden had ever seen; it was gigantic, as big as a bedsheet, and it was *moving* as though it were alive, floating around the girl's figure in a lazy, slow-motion sort of way. The girl was hanging in the air, just above him, and it was the cloak that kept her aloft; the frayed edges of the cloak split into dozens and dozens of long, grasping strips, and these were attached to the fire escape, to the building adjacent the apartment, and to several other spots; the whole arrangement looked something like a big, white spider web, with the girl suspended in the middle of it.

Beneath the rippling cloak, she was wearing a black, jacketed outfit that looked something like a military uniform, with big cuffs and buckles. She was also wearing a rather incongruous-looking pair of sneakers. They looked like Adidas.

Kaden couldn't see the entirety of her face, which was hidden by the cloak's hood, but he could tell from her body language that she wasn't pleased—she had her arms folded over her chest.

Who was she?

"I'll ask again," the girl said, her voice turning a bit dangerous. "Who are you?"

"I might ask you the same thing," Kaden said warily.

The girl moved a bit closer. "I'm the White Ribbon," she said, as if that explained everything.

"I...see."

"That was Joe Arroyo's apartment you just climbed out of," she said, pointing at the window. "He was murdered there last night."

"I'm aware of that."

"What were you doing in there?"

He shrugged. "Just having a look around."

"Who *are* you?"

"I work with Quarterstaff. They call me Skirmish."

"Skirmish?" She snorted. "Never heard of you."

It was mutual, then; Kaden had never heard of *her*, either. Was she a hero? A villain? And what she was doing hanging around a murdered detective's apartment?

"Never heard of me, huh? Unfortunate." He squinted, trying to get a better look at her face, but it was too dark in the alley to make out any detail; everything was soft shadows. "You mind telling me what *you're* doing here?"

"I'm investigating Arroyo's murder."

"Is that so?"

"And you know what? I think I just found myself a suspect." One of the tendril-like strips of her long, frayed cloak began snaking its way toward Kaden—very slowly, very subtly. "I wonder what the police would say," she ventured, "about your sneaking around inside Arroyo's apartment?"

A hero, then. A rookie, probably, who had no idea what she was doing.

"I don't think we need to involve the police."

"I disagree."

He sighed impatiently. "I didn't have anything to do with Arroyo's murder. I've been looking into it myself, for the record; it's possible he was killed by some old friends of mine." He gave her a little goodbye salute. "Now, it was nice meeting you, Miss Ribbon, but if you'll excuse me..."

The tendril drifted closer, undulating through the air like some kind of eel. "You're not going anywhere."

Kaden studied the girl's strange cloak for a moment, wondering how he might go about combatting it. He wasn't particularly intimidated—he'd battled a handful of super-powered men and women before—but the cloak was like nothing he'd ever seen, and he had no idea what it might be capable of. What the hell *was* it, anyway? An alien artifact? Some kind of enchanted object? Hard to guess.

In situations like these, Kaden had found that surprise was a particularly useful tactic; even super-powered beings could sometimes be taken unawares. He glanced up at her, frowning thoughtfully.

"The White Ribbon, huh?"

"That's right."

He nodded appreciatively. "It's got a nice ring to it. I like it."

He gave her a wink...and then, as quick as could be, he drew one of his tonfa and threw it at her.

It was a pretty good throw, and it might have even hit her, had the fantastic cloak not intervened. The long, undulating strip of cloth, the one that had been slowly drifting towards him, reacted instantly to the sudden throw, snatching the tonfa out of the air, cobra-quick, before it had traveled more than ten feet.

And the girl didn't even flinch.

Well, well.

Fortunately he'd only thrown the tonfa to distract her—he didn't want to *fight* this White Ribbon character, or hurt her; he merely wanted to get off the fire escape and get the hell out of there before she could drag him off to the cops. The second after the tonfa left his hand, he vaulted over the fire escape's railing, swung down to the next level, and started running down the stairs.

The girl, still hovering above him, tossed the tonfa away (Kaden heard the clatter as it hit the asphalt) and began lowering herself down to his level. The strips of cloth that had held her in place detached themselves, snaking out and finding new grips as she descended, while the bulk of her cloak opened up, like a parachute, to slow her descent.

That cloak was the damndest thing. It didn't seem to have a fixed size; it had grown immensely to create the parachute, and those tattered, trailing strips of cloth were able to stretch themselves out to seemingly any length. Some of the strips were at least thirty feet along...and some of them were moving in a searching, almost intelligent manner, as though they had minds of their own.

Just what in the hell was he dealing with here?

It didn't take long for the girl to catch up with him; she could descend much faster than he could. "You can't get away from me," she said calmly. "The Ribbon can catch *anything*."

She tilted her head to one side...and almost immediately, several strips of shredded cloth sliddered out of her cloak and darted out in his direction.

The ragged, tentacle-like strips moved very, very quickly, but not quite so quickly that he couldn't follow them. Ducking, dodging, twisting, and turning, all the while acrobatting his way down the fire escape, Kaden found that he was *just* able to avoid the ribbons, though they followed him relentlessly. There were three above, three coming up from below, and two more trying to grab at his wrists from behind; he was forced to trapeze his way all around the fire escape, using the rusted metal like monkey bars, in order to evade them. It reminded him a little of his early Academy training—one of Patch's favorite exercises had been to place his students in the middle of a jungle gym and throw feathered darts at them, while exhorting them to escape.

Kaden's trapeze act brought him all the way down to the third floor. Several of the strips, following his contortions as they chased after him, had gotten themselves tangled up in the fire escape, above *and* below, but there were at least three or four still pursuing him, and the girl was still following him down the side of the building.

"You're fast," she commented, conversationally.

She was only about seven or eight feet away from him. Suddenly inspired, he abruptly decided on another surprise attack: spinning around, he turned, jumped over the fire escape's railing, and flung himself at her.

The girl shrieked, and this time she *did* flinch, but once again, the cloak protected her, whirling around to her front and puffing itself up like a blowfish. Kaden struck the giant bubble and bounced off, but was able to stop his fall by twisting his body around, catlike, and grabbing hold of one of the rungs of the fire escape. From here, he brachiated over to the stairs and dropped down onto another landing. In a moment he was off the fire escape, and safe and sound (well, sound, anyway) on the street.

Above him, the giant white bubble that had enveloped the girl deflated. Spotting him on the street, she lowered herself down, surrounded by those snaking, searching strips of cloth.

"You're *not* getting away," she said.

"I didn't have anything to do with Arroyo's murder," Kaden insisted. "You're wasting your time." He paused for a moment, then added, "I don't want to hurt you."

She snorted at him again. "As if you could."

Annoyed—the adrenaline was really starting to flow now—he pulled his other tonfa out of its sheath and dropped into a fighting stance. "I don't *want* to hurt you," he said, "but if I have to..."

The girl tilted her head a second time...and the cloak's streamer-like appendages suddenly shot out once again, grabbing for him. He charged ahead—evading the ribbons, as he'd evaded them on the fire escape, by leaping all about, performing butterfly twists and aerial somersaults. It was difficult, *really* difficult, but...

He was closing in on her. Twenty feet...ten feet...

But the closer he got, the more strips seemed to appear, and the more trouble he had dodging them. Finally, one of the damned things managed to slither around his ankle and yank him off his feet; he fell on his back, and before he could roll away a half-dozen other tentacles wrapped themselves around his legs and his wrists and dragged him towards the girl.

"You're fast," she repeated, leaning over him. "I'm surprised the Ribbon let you get that close."

He gave the tentacles a couple of experimental tugs, to get a sense of how strong they were. There *was* some give in them—they had a kind of rubbery, elastic feel—but they'd wrapped themselves *very* tightly around his limbs, so tightly that they were cutting off the circulation, and he didn't think he stood much chance of escaping their grip.

He turned his gaze upward, to glare at the girl.

"Now, let's see who we're dealing with..." She leaned down even further, as one of the strips began slithering towards his face. He tried to pull away, but the ribbons held him down, on his knees.

The weird, sinuous fabric slipped beneath his mask, and pulled it off.

Damn.

To his surprise, the girl, upon seeing his uncovered face, gasped and put a hand to her mouth. Had she...recognized him?

Well, regardless, she was distracted, and Kaden had been trained to take advantage of distracted opponents. He didn't think he could overpower her, but maybe...

I've shown you mine. It's only fair I get to see yours.

He gave the ribbon holding his right arm a good, solid jerk, loosening its hold just a *little*...and then spun his tonfa around by the handle, into a *gyakute* grip, and used its long end to catch the hood of her cloak and flip it up, revealing her face.

And now it was Kaden's turn to gasp.

...Because the girl standing in front of him was none other than Isidora Rushforth.

The girl was apoplectic. "You...how did you...?" And without another word, she threw her hood back over her face, released him, and fled back into the darkness of the alley, her cloak trailing after her.

Kaden, now free, slowly rose to his feet, rubbing the circulation back into his wrists.

Izzy Rushforth? Really? *Really?*

He shook his head in astonishment. What were the odds?

CHAPTER FOUR

Kaden made it back to the Daniels Tower just a little after midnight. After taking off his costume and returning his gear to his bedroom closet, he grabbed a bottle of Kayo from the fridge—he had a weakness for the chocolate drink—and went out to the balcony to think.

He was, truth be told, a little distraught. The only person in Signal City who'd known that Kaden Ely was a superhero—that he was *Skirmish*—was Quentin, and the fact that someone else had his secret now was...well, it was unsettling. He didn't *think* Izzy Rushforth would expose him—after all, he had *her* secret now, too, which was good leverage—but he didn't *know* Izzy, and he didn't trust her.

He sighed. Some heroes managed to keep their secrets for years, even decades. Epee, Hammerlock, Mr. Infinity, and the first Midnight Rider had all had very long careers, and had even managed to *retire*, without anyone ever discovering their secret identities. Kaden had slipped up after just ten months.

Quentin was going to be pissed.

Sighing again, he sat down heavily on one of the outdoor chairs, trying to decide how to proceed.

Izzy Rushforth. He didn't know much about the Rushforths, apart from the fact that they were super-rich and owned some kind of giant company. How in the world had their daughter managed to get her hands on that bizarre cloak? How long had she been running around as a superhero? Why was she looking into Joe Arroyo's murder? And why would *anyone* who possessed that kind of power allow herself to be bullied, by the likes of Angel Middleford?

He had a lot of questions. Ordinarily he'd probably try investigating the girl, surreptitiously, as Skirmish—tailing her, studying up on her family business, making some inquiries as to how long she'd been an active crime-fighter and where she might have gotten her cloak—but that approach felt rather needlessly complicated; after all, she sat right next to him in his history class.

The direct approach, he decided, was probably his best bet.

He took a swig of Kayo.

Tomorrow.

* * *

He sought her out the following morning, finding her at her locker just as she was loading up on the books for her first class. "We need to talk," he said flatly.

She turned to look at him. A bit of panic flashed across her face, but she quickly mastered it. "Oh," she said, trying to sound nonchalant. "It's *you*."

"Yeah, it's me." He looked around to see if anyone was listening, then leaned in close. "You know the old storeroom on the second floor? I'll meet you there at three o'clock."

"What for?"

"I told you," he said. "We need to talk."

"I don't think we have anything to talk about." She hesitated. "Except...I'm sorry I accused you of Arroyo's murder. That was a mistake."

He raised an eyebrow. "Oh?"

"I looked you up after I got home last night—I saw the footage of your fight with Wrathbone. You really *are* Quarterstaff's sidekick."

"Not so loud."

"So I apologize for that, for accusing you, but I don't think we have anything else to discuss, and I think...I think we'd be better off if we just stayed out of each other's way from now on." She closed her locker and started to walk away.

He caught her wrist. "I have *questions*," he growled into her ear.

"If you want me to stay out of your way, I'll stay out of your way, but first we're gonna put all our cards on the table. I want your story, and I want to know what *you* know about Arroyo's murder. I can tell you what little *I* know, if you're interested. We can help each other out. All right?"

She looked down at his hand, the one holding on to her wrist. "Fine," she harrumphed, after a moment. "Three o'clock." And with that, she shook her arm free and proceeded down the hallway...without looking back.

* * *

Izzy may have been brusque, but she was, at least, punctual; she opened the door to the storeroom and peeked inside at precisely three o'clock. Kaden was already there, waiting for her.

"Hi," he greeted.

"Hi," she replied, unenthusiastically. She entered the room and closed the door behind her. "You're sure no one's going to bother us in here?"

"Pretty sure." He decided to get right to the point. "How long have you been the White Ribbon?"

She frowned at his directness, but answered readily enough. "Since April."

"Six months, huh? Seen any action?" He sat down on a table, legs dangling.

"I had a run-in with Ruby Laser around the Fourth of July," she said. "She...got away."

"That's all?"

Her eyes narrowed. "I got a couple of Ma Crime's goons arrested, after I caught them harassing a hot dog vendor on King Island. And I've run down plenty of muggers and car thieves." She sounded a bit defensive. "What about *you*? How long have you been Quarterstaff's sidekick?"

"Not quite a year."

"Where'd you learn all that martial arts stuff? Did Quarterstaff teach you?"

It was his turn to frown. "Not...exactly. I was a student at the Matsumoto Academy."

Her eyes went wide. "The Matsumoto Academy? Aren't they a

bunch of assassins or something?"

"Sort of. The Academy is a sort of underground martial arts school. It's where the Dark train their operatives."

"The Dark?"

"An organized crime outfit. Came out of Japan, originally. The boss, Sho Matsumoto—they call him the Darkest—is the great-great grandson of the man who started the group, back in the 1850's. They've been around a long time."

"And you...were one of them? An assassin?"

"They're not *all* assassins. And not all of the Academy's students go on to work for the Dark—they'll train anyone who can afford it. You ever heard of Missy Mischief? Her real name's Yvette Lemieux; she's from New Orleans. She got *her* training at the Academy. So did Damon Rake, and Kilkenny, although Kilkenny washed out after a few months. The training's pretty tough."

"How did you end up there?"

"My uncle worked for the Dark." He shrugged. "They saw something in me, I guess, some potential. So they started training me. There were six in my class; I was the youngest. Seven years old." He shook his head, dismissing the memories. "Enough about me. I want to hear about that cloak of yours. What is it? And where did you get it?"

She didn't answer right away. "It's...it's a long story."

"You don't want to tell me."

"I don't think it's any of your business. But..." She sighed. "Okay. If you must know...it was a gift."

"So who gave it to you?"

"I don't know who she was. I was out shopping one day, in Shanghai—I was on vacation there with my parents—when a strange old woman approached me and handed me this small wooden box, painted red. She told me the Ribbon was inside, and that it was magic, and that..." She trailed off, her eyes taking on a faraway look. "And that it was my destiny to be a hero."

"Your destiny?"

"That's what she told me."

"I see," he said, trying to keep the skepticism out of his voice. "It's a magical artifact, then?"

"That's right."

That made sense. Kaden didn't know the first thing about magic, but there was certainly plenty of it to go around in Signal City; several superheroes made use of mystical artifacts, and there were several full-blown sorcerers active in the city as well. Enchantryn, for instance, one of the super-powered Paranormals, was widely believed to be the second or third most powerful magic-worker in the world.

"How does it work?" he asked. "Do you control it, or does it act independently? I got the impression last night that it was sort of...alive."

"I think it is, in a way. I can control it, with my thoughts, but it also acts on its own sometimes."

"Like when I jumped at you?"

She nodded. "It protects me. And it's *very* good protection. It's bulletproof, you know."

"Interesting." He fixed her with a steady gaze. "Who else knows?"

"That I'm the White Ribbon?" She shook her head. "You're the only one. I haven't told anybody, not even my parents...and *you'd* better not tell anybody, either."

"I can keep a secret," Kaden said nonchalantly. "Can you?"

She shrugged. "I don't have any reason to expose you."

"Good. I'll hold you to that. And now that we have all *that* settled..." He clapped his hands together. "What do you know about Joe Arroyo?"

"Not much," she admitted.

He raised an eyebrow. "I thought you said you were investigating his murder."

"I am, but I'd never even heard of him until a few weeks ago. He was the lead detective on a case I've been working on."

"The stolen weapons, you mean?"

She looked confused. "Stolen weapons? I don't know anything about that. What *I'm* working on is a kidnapping case."

Kaden scratched his chin thoughtfully. "A kidnapping?"

"A thirteen-year-old girl. Her name is Olivia Pottinger. She ran away from home back in June and hasn't been seen since. It's believed she was abducted."

He nodded slowly. "I think I might have seen something about that on TV."

"It was pretty big news for a while," she confirmed. "Olivia came from a very old, very wealthy family; the Pottingers owned half of Signal City back in the day. My parents were acquainted with *her* parents, and I knew her slightly—I'd seen her at parties and stuff. After she disappeared...well, I decided I'd try to find her." Her face took on a pained expression. "Her parents...if you'd seen the looks on her parents' faces..."

"And Arroyo was investigating her abduction?"

"Yes."

"Had he made any progress?"

She shook her head. "I don't really know. I never met him, never talked to him. I'd seen his name in the papers, though, and after he was murdered..." She put up a palm. "I got suspicious, so I flew over to his apartment to see what I could see. That's when I ran into you."

"You can fly?"

"It's more like gliding, actually. What was that about stolen weapons before?"

"Oh. Well, the stolen weapons are the reason *I* was looking into his murder. Arroyo was also investigating a series of thefts, of some strange, supernatural weapons—swords, daggers, things like that. There's a good chance the Dark is responsible; they like unusual weapons. Sho Matsumoto has a whole collection of them. Anyway, it's looking to me like the Dark had him killed, after he started connecting the dots on whatever they were up to."

"Are you sure?"

"Am I sure the Dark had him killed? Not entirely, but there's plenty of circumstantial evidence. He *was* stabbed, you know; that's kind of a giveaway. The Dark's assassins have always been partial to swords and knives. They're an old-fashioned bunch."

She absorbed all that. "Too bad."

"What's too bad?"

"I thought Arroyo's murder might have had something to do with Olivia's kidnapping. It was a long shot, but..." She sighed. "I've hit a dead end."

"How long ago did you say she was abducted?"

"It's been about four months."

Kaden puffed out a little breath. "Four months is a long time for a little girl to be missing," he said doubtfully. "You don't have any other leads?"

"No. They found one of her shoes outside the Doyle Street Station—that's where the kidnapping seems to have taken place—

and a knife, as well, but that's all."

"A knife?"

She nodded. "A knife with some blood on it. The blood belonged to Olivia."

"That doesn't sound promising." The girl, Kaden decided, had almost certainly been murdered, but he didn't think that was something Izzy wanted to hear.

"I know." She looked at him defiantly. "But I'm not giving up."

He regarded her curiously. "You know, I'm usually pretty good at reading people, but I don't think I would've ever guessed that you were a superhero. The way you let Angel Middleford and her gang walk all over you..."

"Angel's an idiot."

"So why do you let her bully you?"

"I..." She turned away from him. "It's a disguise."

"A disguise?"

"You said it yourself. No one would ever believe that a poor, bullied girl was actually a superhero. Besides...I'm used to being bullied."

"I don't think anyone ever gets used to having chocolate pudding dumped on their heads."

"It's always been like that. People...people think I have it all, because I've got pretty hair and because my family has so much money. They think people like me ought to be happy, and friendly, and smiling all the time, because we're so...so fortunate. But that's not me. I'm not that way. I've *never* been that way. So people like Angel get it in their heads that I must be a huge snob, because I keep to myself and don't give them their stupid smiles all the time."

Kaden wasn't sure if he bought all that—the "disguise" explanation seemed especially dubious—but he let it slide. "If you say so. Haven't you ever been tempted to put her in her place, though, with the Ribbon? Or don't you bring the Ribbon to school?"

"Of course I bring it to school." She rolled up one of the sleeves of her blue blazer, revealing a white band wrapped around her forearm. "I never take it off."

"That's it?" he asked. "That's the Ribbon?"

"It shrinks. But to answer your question...of *course* I'm tempted. I don't *like* having idiots like Angel dumping pudding on my head. But I'm...I'm used to it."

"You said that already."

She seemed to collect herself. "Well, it's true," she huffed. "And anyway, using the Ribbon to scare Angel would give me away. I don't want anyone finding out I'm a superhero. It's bad enough that *you* found out."

He smirked. "Sorry."

"I guess we're done here," she continued, turning to leave. "See you in class."

"See you," he said, sliding off the table. "Say, if you need any help on that kidnapping case—"

"No thanks. It's like I said before—I think we'd be better off staying out of each other's way."

"Why?"

"I...I work alone."

"I'm a bit of a loner myself," Kaden admitted. "But sometimes two heads are better than one. Working with Quarterstaff taught me that. If you *really* want to find this girl..."

She stopped at the doorway. "I *will* find her," she said determinedly, her hands clenching into fists. She gave Kaden a backwards glance. "Thanks, though. Thanks for the offer."

And she left.

Strange girl, Kaden thought. She *did* have pretty hair, though.

CHAPTER FIVE

*K*aden stayed home that night, but went out the next, as Skirmish. It was a pleasant, late-September night in Signal City. The autumn weather had, at last, taken the edge off the summer heat; every evening, now, seemed to be just a bit cooler than the last, and the city was seeing more and more rainy days as well. Winter was on its way.

Quentin usually went out as Quarterstaff three or four times a week, depending on what he was working on. On slow nights, he hopped on his matte-black Harley Nightster and made a circuit around downtown Signal City, starting in Liberty Park and heading all the way down to Wellington before turning north and driving back to the Daniels Tower. Kaden would typically follow him on his own motorcycle, on those slow nights, but when he was on his own, as he was tonight, he preferred to avoid downtown—there were already a lot of heroes operating there, and he didn't think the big guys (the CrossGuard, the Quantum Man, Overclocked, and all the rest) needed any help from him. So he hit the shadier neighborhoods instead—southern Stone's Row, Friars, and sometimes even Steelworks. There was *always* something shady happening in Steelworks. Unfortunately the Barathrum Bridge, which linked Signal City to the Steelworks peninsula, had been destroyed by the Supreme Saboteur earlier that summer, and the only other way into the crime-prone neighborhood was through Lowtown, via South Bridge. And that was a long, long way to drive.

So he stuck to Stone's Row, trawling through the back alleys, looking for trouble. The northern portion of Stone's Row was heavily gentrified, but its southern outskirts, below 49th, were dark and dangerous, and it didn't take long for Kaden to find a fight: around eleven o'clock he batted around a couple of would-be liquor store thieves, and about an hour after that he took on a couple of aggressive, long-haired cultists—acolytes of the local crime boss/brainwasher who called himself the Neo-Rasputin.

None of the crooks he encountered presented much of a challenge. The liquor store thieves were worthless brawlers, helpless without their guns, and the cultists were so awkward, in their stupid robes, that it had taken only a moment for Kaden to knock them off their feet and tie them up for the cops.

Brief fights. Fun, though, while they'd lasted.

He'd just put the finishing touches on the cultists, and was making his way back to his motorcycle, when he suddenly got the feeling that he was being watched. Frowning, he stopped to survey the dark, narrow street in which he'd parked his bike.

Probably just my imagin–

All at once, a fist blasted out of the shadows, from behind, whiffing by his left ear. Instinctively, he jerked his head to the right and batted the arm away with the back of his hand, then ducked, spun on his heel, and sprang back a step, his fists up and ready to box.

"Slick," an amused voice said. "You've still got it, kid."

Kaden lowered his fists. He *knew* that voice. "Sly?"

The man stepped out of the shadows. "Nice to see you, Kaden. It's been...what? Four years? Five?"

"At least," Kaden said cautiously. Sly had been one of his instructors at the Matsumoto Academy. A friendly, easygoing fellow, Sly—unlike most of the other instructors—had never beaten or abused his students, had seemed to enjoy getting to know them, and had managed to instill, in Kaden at least, a genuine love for the martial arts. That was probably why the Dark had dismissed him; Sly just wasn't ruthless enough. He'd left the syndicate about a year before Kaden's own departure.

"Sorry about the sneak attack," he said, grinning. "Just a bit of fun. I see you haven't forgotten *everything* I taught you."

"Sly..." Seeing the man now, for the first time in years, was flabbergasting, and was filling him up with old, long-forgotten feelings and emotions. For better or worse, the men and women of the Academy had been his family for seven years, and Sly...Sly had been like an uncle, or maybe even a father. He'd taught Kaden how to think, how to fight, how to use his tonfa; how to look for flaws in a style; how to read a man's eyes; how to ignore the taunts of the older students, when they teased and bullied him; how to be confident, how to stand up straight; and how important it was to keep going, to keep fighting, even when the odds seemed impossible.

It was surreal, seeing the man again. And the fact that he obviously knew Kaden's secret...well, that was even *more* disconcerting.

Sly chuckled at his discomfiture. "Surprised, eh? I guess I should've expected that."

"It's...it's good to see you, too, Sly." His teacher hadn't changed much over the past five years; he still looked like an over-the-hill boy-bander, with fun-loving eyes and a seemingly perpetual five o'clock shadow. His brown hair was a carefully-tousled mess.

"Likewise." He gave the seat of Kaden's motorcycle a little pat. "Nice bike. Yamaha FZ8, isn't it? How long have you had it?"

"Well, it's...it's not really mine."

"Oh. Belongs to Daniels, huh?"

Kaden stared. "You...you know?"

"That Quentin Daniels is Quarterstaff? And that you're his sidekick?" He nodded. "Wasn't too hard to figure out. I caught a few of your fights on YouTube; your style gave you away. I was the one who taught you those tonfa tricks, remember?" He chuckled again. "And after I found out you were taken in by Quentin Daniels...well, it didn't take a genius."

"I...I..."

Sly put up his hands in a disarming sort of way. "Don't worry, kid. I'm not planning on selling you guys out or anything. If you want to be a superhero now, that's your business." He gave the motorcycle an appreciative look. "Seems like a pretty nice gig."

Kaden crossed his arms and fixed his old teacher with a hard look. "What's going on here, Sly? Why'd you track me down?"

He shrugged. "Friendly chat? I thought you might want to get a cup of coffee–"

"Try again."

He laughed immediately. "No, you're right; this isn't a social call." His voice turned serious. "I've been searching for you for the past two months, kid...to warn you."

"Warn me?"

"Rio's back in town."

Kaden took a deep breath. "And?"

"And he's after you. He's been doing wetwork for the Dark."

Hearing Rio's name had triggered another avalanche of mixed-up feelings and emotions. Rio Killian had been his best friend at the Academy. For seven years, for seven *long* years, they'd laughed together, trained together, and fought together. Both had been orphans, handed over to the Dark at a young age; both had grown into preternaturally skilled martial artists. Rio was...well, if Sly had been an uncle, Rio had been a brother.

Their friendship had been part rivalry, of course—the Academy's instructors liked to encourage rivalries between their students—and in the end, the rivalry had destroyed the friendship, but for seven years Rio had been one of the most important people in Kaden's life.

You can run away from us, Rio had told him, as the blood and the rain had mingled together. *But you can't run away from yourself.*

His old rival had left Signal City three years ago, to complete his training overseas. Kaden had hoped he'd seen the last of him, but...

"Rio, huh?"

"I'm afraid so."

"What makes you think he's coming after me?"

"It's what I've been hearing. I've been out of the business a long time, but I still know some people in the organization. They give me updates, sometimes."

Kaden looked at him curiously. "What do you do for a living now, anyway?"

He grinned. "Real estate."

"Really?"

"Really."

He considered all this for a moment or two. "So...Rio's been doing assassinations for the Dark."

"That's right."

"Do you have any names?"

"No, but my contacts tell me he specializes in law enforcement hits." He made an exasperated sort of noise. "You remember Rio. He never did like cops."

Kaden blinked. "Sly...have you ever heard of a guy named Joe Arroyo?"

He shook his head. "No. Who is he?"

"A detective. Murdered in his apartment a few days ago. It looked like a syndicate job to me; Arroyo had been investigating some robberies that the Dark might have had something to do with."

"Ah." He nodded. "Yeah. It's possible they gave that hit to Rio. How was it done?"

"Looked like a sword to me."

He grunted. "Butterfly swords, I'll bet. I never should've taught him how to use those things."

Kaden sighed. *Great. Just great.*

"So what are these robberies all about?" Sly asked.

"What? Oh...just a little case Quentin and I have been working on. Someone's been going around stealing antique weapons—some with magical properties. It looks like the Dark's work."

"I see. Well, I wouldn't be surprised; Sho's always had a thing for antiques."

"These contacts of yours haven't mentioned anything about these thefts, have they?"

"Haven't heard anything."

"Shame." He looked at his old teacher thoughtfully. "Real estate? Really?"

"Turns out I have a knack for it. I've got property in Lowtown, Friars...some in Stone's Row, but the market's getting a bit too tricky for me up here, what with all the yuppies moving in." He dismissed the digression with a wave. "Listen, Kaden, about Rio..."

"You wouldn't happen to know where I could find him, would you?"

Sly frowned. "No, and I wouldn't tell you if I did. I don't want to see you get killed, kid. Hell, that's why I went to the trouble of tracking you down."

"I can handle Rio."

"I wonder. I know the two of you were always pretty evenly matched, back in school, but Rio's a *professional* now, kid. He's a killer. He won't have any trouble pulling that trigger." He gave his former student a meaningful look. "When's the last time *you* killed a man?"

Kaden said nothing.

"I thought so." He wagged a finger at him. "Watch yourself, kid. Watch your back." He pulled a notepad out of his pocket and scribbled something down on it. "Here," he said, handing it to Kaden. "My cell number, if you'd like to get in touch with me. If I hear anything else about what Rio's up to...I don't know, maybe I can help you out."

He turned away—disappearing, once more, into the shadows.

"Thanks, Sly," Kaden called after him. "Thanks for the heads-up."

"Least I could do," he replied, "for my favorite student."

* * *

Kaden called it a night after that, hopping on his motorcycle and returning to the Daniels Tower. His thoughts were full of the past: Sly, teaching him how to catch a sword with a tonfa; long, grueling sparring sessions in decaying mansions and darkened warehouses; the night he'd sneaked out of his barracks, with Rio, to see a movie; and the night Fan had told him, very calmly and conversationally, that his uncle John, his only family, had been murdered.

That had been the last straw; he'd left the Academy the next day. Rio had begged him to stay, following him into the storm...

Halloween night.

He shook his head—trying, in vain, to dismiss the thoughts. But they bubbled back up, again and again.

Arriving home, he stashed his gear and went out to the balcony to brood. The view was lovely; downtown Signal City, after dark, was a forest of tall, shadowy skyscrapers, lit by those thousands and thousands of multicolored lights. There was always something to see out there.

He was just settling down with another bottle of chocolate Kayo when, to his astonishment, a huge, white bird, coming up from below, suddenly burst into view directly in front of him and landed lightly on the balcony's railing. Alarmed, he started at the sight, and at the accompanying rush of wind...only to realize, after a second or two, that the bird *wasn't* a bird—it was Izzy Rushforth, wrapped up in her magical Ribbon. The cloak was enormous, the size of a hang glider, but was already shrinking; by the time she hopped off the balcony railing, and landed on the deck, it was no bigger than an ordinary cloak.

"Hi," she greeted, throwing back her hood.

"Hi," Kaden replied, a bit warily. "How did you get all the way up here?"

"Thermal."

"Huh. Impressive." He studied her for a second, then added, "I suppose the next question is, *what* are you doing here?"

"I need to talk to you."

His eyes narrowed. "You know, I don't recall ever giving you my address. How did you–"

"It was pretty obvious. The rumor around school is you're related to Quentin Daniels–"

"We're *not* related. Quentin adopted me."

"Well, regardless, I did a little research, and..." She looked at him carefully. "Quentin Daniels...he's Quarterstaff, isn't he?"

Kaden sighed irritably. Far too many people had been deducing his—and Quentin's—secrets lately. It was starting to get annoying. "Yes."

"Thought so."

"You said you needed my help?" he asked, impatient.

"Oh. Yes."

"I thought you preferred to work alone."

"I do. It's just...I've been thinking about what you said, about two heads being better than one." She fidgeted a bit. "The important thing is finding Olivia. I shouldn't let my pride, or anything else, get in the way of that. If you *can* help me..."

He nodded in understanding. "All right. What do you need?"

"I learned something about Joe Arroyo this afternoon," she said, beginning to pace along the length of the balcony. "Apparently, a few days before he was murdered, he went down into the sewers and had some kind of meeting with the Eyeball."

"The Eyeball?" The Eyeball, whose real name was Phinneas Eyling, was an eccentric superhero, close to retirement age, who lived in the labyrinthine sewer network beneath Signal City. He was a gadget-man, who owned a whole arsenal of strange devices; Kaden had met him a few times on adventures with Quentin. "What kind of meeting?"

"I don't know, but I think it might have had something to do with Olivia's kidnapping. The Eyeball may have seen something, heard something. I'd like to talk to him."

"So talk to him."

"I don't know how to *find* him. That's why I'm here. I know you've fought sewer monsters before—guys like Wrathbone—and I thought...I thought maybe you knew your way around down there. Could you take me to him?"

Kaden *did* have some familiarity with the sewers, and he nodded affirmatively. "I think so. He has a couple of different hideouts, but I think I could find him if I had to." His eyes fell on her white Adidas. "I wouldn't wear *those* into the sewers, though. You'll need to find some rubber boots."

She looked down at her shoes. "You're probably right."

"Where'd you get that costume, anyway? It looks like some kind of anime cosplay."

"I made it," she said defensively. "I sewed it up myself. What, you think *your* costume is something special? It's nothing but body armor." She put her nose up. "And all that black makes you look like a bad guy."

"Whatever," he grumbled. "So when do you want to see the Eyeball?"

"How about this weekend?"

"Fine." With that settled, neither of them really had anything else left to say, and so for a moment they just stood there, awkwardly. Finally, Kaden asked, "Do you want to come inside, or...?"

"No, no, that's okay," she said quickly. "I should get going." She climbed up on the railing. "See you in school." And she jumped off the edge, her cloak expanding into the glider once again.

She floated away, on a warm wind, while Kaden went back to brooding.

CHAPTER SIX

*H*e saw Izzy again the next day, in their history class. "Morning," he said.

She mumbled something in response, but didn't make eye contact and didn't stop to chat. Instead, she found her seat, flipped open her history book, and immediately stuck her nose in it.

He wasn't entirely sure what to make of this discourteousness, but since he wasn't feeling all that chatty himself, he let it slide. He found his own seat (the two of them sat in the back row), opened up his book, and leaned back in his chair, already yawning at the prospect of a full hour spent listening to Mr. Kronkenburger.

Their teacher was a dour-sounding man in his mid-fifties, with salt-and-pepper hair and a penchant for sweater vests. Today he was talking about World War II.

"Signal City, of course, contributed to the war effort in a number of ways," he was saying. "There were many, many munitions factories in Steelworks, and the heroes of the time offered their considerable expertise as well: Albert Stein, who called himself Captain Radar, invented a number of new technologies for the Allies, while the Lantern brothers helped design tanks and planes..."

Kaden was only half-listening when, a few minutes later, Mr. Kronkenburger suddenly sprung an assignment on them. "You'll be pairing up," he said, to the groans of his students, "and giving presentations to the class on this—the United States home front, during the Second World War. Each group will focus on a different aspect of the war effort; I'll be assigning the topics for research." He clapped his hands together. "So, let's get paired up."

And so the students got up and began wandering around the classroom, looking for partners. Kaden rolled his eyes at the exercise; he hated these sorts of assignments.

He glanced over at Izzy, who, like him, had remained seated at her desk. She was twiddling her thumbs, and starting to look a little uncomfortable.

Why not? He slid his desk over an inch or two and leaned over to talk to her. "What do you say? Want to work together?"

"With you?" She hesitated. "I...I don't know."

This surprised him. "Okay..."

"It's just...I think it'd be better if we pretended like we didn't know each other at school."

"Why?"

"Because..." Her shoulders slumped. "It's complicated."

Kaden didn't know what was eating her, but he shrugged it off. "All right, if that's what you want." He slid his desk back. "Maybe Angel Middleford needs a partner..."

"No, no. It's all right. We can do this stupid project together."

They got up and approached Mr. Kronkenburger's desk. He wrote down their names and handed them a sheet of paper. "You'll be discussing the domestic economy," he told them. "Rationing, in particular."

"Sounds fun," Kaden remarked, in a somewhat less than enthusiastic tone.

Mr. Kronkenburger glared at him; apparently the guy didn't have much of a sense of humor. "Perhaps you'd like another assignment, Mr. Ely?"

"No," he said lamely, accepting the sheet of paper. He heard a few snickers from the other students as he returned to his desk, and even Izzy gave him a dark look.

He hated school.

The bell rang a few minutes later. "I'm free next period," Izzy told him, as he got up to leave. "What about you?"

"Yeah, same."

"We should head to the library, then, and start looking for some research material. I'd like to get this out of the way."

Kaden wasn't nearly as sedulous as this—he usually waited until the last minute to do his assignments—but he figured they'd probably both be better off if Izzy took charge of the project, so he gave her a reluctant nod. "Okay," he said, sighing. "Let's go."

The two of them gathered up their backpacks and headed for the library. They found Angel, however, waiting for them in the hallway, with a couple of her mean-girl friends.

"Well, look at this," she said, her voice full of mocking. "Pudding Head's found herself a boyfriend—and he's almost as tall as she is! Cute!"

Kaden was, in fact, probably about an inch taller than Izzy, but he got the dig. "Hilarious. That's hilarious, Angel. Now if you'll excuse us..."

Angel laughed her deep, bellowing laugh (that was a seriously weird voice she had). "Oh, I get it. He's not a boyfriend, he's a *bodyguard*. How much is she paying you, Pee-Wee?"

Her overloud voice was beginning to attract attention; people were stopping to listen to the exchange. Kaden, annoyed (and growing *more* annoyed by the moment), narrowed his eyes at the chubby girl. "What do you want, Angel?"

"From you? Nothing."

"Then get out of my way, you cow. I don't have time for this."

That set her to seething. "You can't talk to me like that," she snarled. "My boyfriend—"

"You seem a little upset," he said calmly. "What's the matter? The farmer forget to feed you this morning?" The crowd laughed at that; Angel turned red.

"You'll pay for that one," she said, through gritted teeth.

"I'm sure. Come on, Izzy, let's get out of—" He turned around, looking for her, only to discover that she'd disappeared into the crowd while he'd been trading barbs with her bully.

This struck Kaden as somewhat ungracious. Where had she run off to? Figuring she might have gone on ahead of him, he pushed his way past the seething Angel and headed to the library...but she wasn't there, either.

He shook his head, exasperated. He was having a hard time figuring this girl out.

* * *

Race made his customary appearance at lunch a few hours later, sitting himself down across from Kaden and immediately opening up an issue of *Aces*, a glossy superhero mag. "Just got it today," he said. "Let's see...new pictures of Shieldmaiden...she got her original shield back a few months ago, did you know that? I heard she went back in time, to before it was destroyed." He flipped a few more pages. "Sky Skater fights Nailgun...Mister Blizzard visits Signal City...Darby Fray joins the Selectmen...oh! Look at this! There's a big article here about the Paranormals. Have you ever seen them? They're based right here in Stone's Row, you know."

"I've seen them around," he said nonchalantly. As a matter of fact he'd helped the superhero team foil one of the Psychoswami's schemes just a few months ago.

"I saw them fighting Goth Chick once, up on 57th. I was in a taxi with my folks. Man! That was something. You ever seen Goth Chick?"

"No."

"I'll find you a picture," he said, picking up his phone.

"That's okay, Race. I'm not that interested."

He put the phone back down, disappointed. "Oh." But he returned to his usual, excitable self a mere moment later: "Ooh, this should be good," he said, continuing to leaf through the magazine. "Some details about what happened in Neptunia while the CrossGuard was down there. They fought the Barbary Lion, did you hear about that? He managed to kidnap Miracle Girl somehow, but her husband—I forget his name; he's some ordinary guy—teamed up with Captain Penrose to rescue her. Say, who do you think would win in a fight between the Barbary Lion and that Viking-guy Bloodbane? I saw his ship on the news the other night–"

"I don't know, Race," he sighed, picking at his food.

The kid studied him. "Hey...you're looking a little down. What's the matter?"

"Nothing. It's just...I've got a lot going on."

"I heard you got into it with Angel this morning."

He grunted an affirmative.

"It's about time *someone* stood up to her." He shivered. "And better you than me."

He shook his head. "Angel Middleford's the least of my

43

problems." When Race gave him a questioning look, he added, "There's this kid I used to know, back at my old school. He was a friend once, a good friend, but now...well, let's just say we're not on very good terms anymore. I'm just wondering where we went wrong." He picked at his food some more. "I've been thinking about the past a lot lately."

Race nodded slowly. "People drift apart sometimes," he said. "Back in elementary school I used to be really good friends with this girl—Mei was her name. We played video games together, and watched anime, and read *Little Champions* on the way home from school. Man, was she cute." He smiled a little at the memories.

"So what happened?"

"She grew up. Started hanging out with the girls. In the fifth grade she just stopped talking to me. I wasn't all that popular, and I think...I think maybe I'd started to embarrass her."

Race wasn't all that good at hiding his feelings on his face—he was a completely guileless sort of person—and Kaden could see the hurt reflected there. "I'm sorry," he said. "You didn't deserve that."

"It happens," he said, returning to his magazine. "Like I said, people drift apart, and for all kinds of reasons. Maybe this friend of yours just turned into a jerk. *That* happens sometimes, too. Anyway, I wouldn't let it bother you."

Kaden gave him a sympathetic smile. "Thanks, Race," he said, getting up to leave. "Nice talking to you." He paused, and then added, "See you tomorrow?"

The kid's eyes lit up. "Yeah! Of course. I'll be here."

* * *

He ran into Izzy in the hallway a few hours later, at the end of the school day. "What happened to you this morning?" he demanded. "I thought we were going to the library."

"Sorry," she said, though she didn't actually *sound* all that contrite. "I *did* go to the library later, though—I checked out some books we can use."

"Okaaay, but why did you leave me hanging like that?"

She shrugged. "I don't know. I just didn't want to get mixed up in another big scene with Angel. She went after me at lunch a few days ago; the whole dining hall heard–"

"I thought you said you were used to being bullied."

She glowered at him. "I didn't say I *liked* it. Look, sometimes...sometimes it's just better to leave trouble alone, okay?"

Kaden couldn't believe what he was hearing. "Are you kidding me? You're a *superhero*, Izzy. Superheroes are supposed to go out *looking* for trouble."

She whirled on him. "I'm *not* a superhero," she hissed. "Not here." She held up a pair of fingers. "Izzy Rushforth and the White Ribbon are two different people, Kaden. *Two*."

He was puzzled. "I don't get it. Are you saying the Ribbon takes over your body or something? That it has its own personality?"

"No, of course not. What I'm saying is...I'm not the same..." But she trailed off there, apparently at a loss for words. She shook her head in frustration. "I've gotta go."

Kaden threw up his hands. "Whatever. You still on for heading into the sewers this weekend?"

"Yes, yes. Where do you want to meet?"

He thought about it. "There's an entrance into the downtown system behind the old Barnes Theater, over on Xerxes. You know where that is?"

"I think so."

"Okay. I'll be there at ten o'clock, on Saturday night."

"Ten o'clock. Got it." And she hurried off.

Still a little exasperated, Kaden watched her run off, her white-blonde hair bouncing along on her shoulders. *Strange girl.*

Putting his hands in his pockets, he turned around there and headed for the building's exit. He'd just pushed open the front doors, and begun making his way down the front steps, when an angry voice suddenly called out to him.

"Hey! Ely!"

He turned. The voice, he quickly discovered, belonged to a fellow student—Russell Lachmiller, a senior, who happened to be the captain of the school's wrestling team. He was a huge, hulking beast, well over two hundred pounds, with a shaved head and a heavy brow; his uniform made him look like a dressed-up caveman. He was almost a full foot taller than Kaden.

He'd taken off his blazer, and was rolling up the sleeves of his button-up shirt.

Angel and her gal-pals were there, too, already giggling at the proceedings.

Hmm...

"I wanna talk to you," Russell grunted, stomping over to him.

"All right," he said casually, setting his backpack down. "How can I help you, Russell?"

"You can apologize," he said, "to my girl."

He raised an eyebrow. "Your girl?"

The big guy jerked a thumb over his shoulder, at Angel. "Oh," Kaden said, looking past him. "Your girl."

"Apology. Let's hear it."

He looked up at the beefy senior, his eyes narrowing. "You know what, Russell? I'm not really in an apologizing mood."

The beast cracked his knuckles. "All right. You had your chance."

Kaden grinned despite himself; the prospect of a fight with this brute was already getting his blood up. Here, he decided, was an opportunity to blow off a little steam...and, perhaps, to get Angel Middleford and her girl gang off his back for once and for all.

He gave the giant an appraising look, taking note of his height, and his reach, and of how he was carrying his weight. Russell was a wrestler, and Kaden suspected that he would probably fight like one; he'd come at him in a rush and try to drag him down to the ground, where his great weight and superior strength would provide him with a tremendous advantage. Kaden couldn't allow that to happen; all the martial arts skills in the world wouldn't mean a thing if this giant managed to get him off his feet. He would have to keep his distance.

He'd fought grapplers before, though, and he wasn't too worried.

"Let's do this, then," Kaden said. He took a step back...

...And Russell attacked, in exactly the way Kaden had predicted he would. Charging forward (and he was a lot faster than he looked) he threw both arms out and grabbed for him, grasping for his clothes, his arms, anything he could get ahold of. Anticipating this, Kaden backed up, hopped up on the cement railing that ran along the school's front steps, and somersaulted right over his head.

Russell spun around. If he was impressed by Kaden's gymnastics, he didn't show it; he charged him again, shoulder-forward, like a linebacker. Kaden had the space he needed to deliver a strike now, however, and just as the beast was closing in, he turned his back to him and caught him with a simple mule kick. The back of his heel struck the senior in the face, hard, snapping his head back and stopping him dead in his tracks.

Russell was a big, angry guy, though, and just now he was full of adrenaline. Recovering quickly (though blood was pouring out of his nose, all over his white shirt), he abandoned the wrestling tactics and tried throwing a couple of awkward haymakers instead. Kaden, still wary of getting caught in a takedown, avoided these, dancing around him from a distance.

By now a crowd had gathered—a pretty large one—and chants of "Fight! Fight!" were filling the air. As the obvious underdog, most of the students seemed to be supporting Kaden, despite the efforts of Angel and her friends to cheerlead for Russell.

Kaden wasn't listening to the cheers, though; he was concentrating on finding an opening. The big guy was too tall to hit with a good counterpunch to the face, he mused, but his midsection was unprotected. Maybe...

Nodding to himself, he dodged a few more big haymakers, then dropped *below* one, slipped inside Russell's guard, and hit him in the kidneys with a very hard, extended-knuckle thrust-punch.

And *that* ended the fight. Russell, practically screaming in agony, fell sideways onto the steps, clutching his side. The blood was still burbling out of his nose.

The crowd was impressed. Angel, naturally, was appalled.

Annoyed that the big fellow hadn't given him a better fight, Kaden gave him a contemptuous little kick as he walked past him, on his way to retrieve his backpack. "Pleasure doing business with you," he deadpanned. "Next time–"

"Hey! What's going on here?"

Mr. Kronkenburger had just emerged from the school. Seeing Kaden standing above the defeated, blood-soaked Russell, was all the evidence he needed: "You! Ely! Come with me!"

Kaden spread his hands and tried to look innocent. "I was only defending–"

"*Now!*"

CHAPTER SEVEN

*T*he Barnes Theater was a grand old building, recently renovated, which occupied a whole corner at the end of Xerxes Avenue in western Stone's Row. The surrounding neighborhood was a little sketchy, full of dark, claustrophobic alleys and graffitied buildings, but the yuppies were working on it; in recent years a big shopping district had emerged just a few blocks to the north, and there were brightly-lit bars and nightclubs running all along nearby Darius Avenue to the east.

Kaden preferred the sketchiness.

He didn't have to wait long for Izzy to show up; she appeared just a few minutes after ten, swinging into view via those long, trailing ribbons of cloth. "I don't like these narrow alleys," she said, upon landing. "There's not enough room to glide. Hi, Kaden."

"*Skirmish*," he corrected, tapping at his mask.

"Oh. Right." She frowned. "How did you get that name, anyway?"

"Quarterstaff gave it to me," he replied, shrugging. "I like to fight. I'm *always* fighting."

She studied him. "Yeah. I heard you beat up Russell Lachmiller yesterday."

"He had it coming." He gave her a sidelong glance. "Angel put him up to it, you know."

"I had a feeling," she said quietly. "I'm sorry about—"

"Don't be sorry. It wasn't *your* fault, and the guy really *did* have it coming. Maybe next time he'll think twice about picking on a guy half his size."

"So did you get in trouble?"

He nodded. "They suspended me."

Her mouth fell open. "What? Really?"

"I broke the guy's nose. Of *course* they suspended me."

"But didn't he start it?"

He chuckled. "Nobody cares who *started* it. Besides, I've got a record; I've been suspended for fighting before. Easier to blame me for the whole thing."

"You've been suspended before?"

"Couple of times. My first year at Jeffries was pretty rough. Coming out of the Matsumoto Academy was...well, I had to make some adjustments."

"Aren't you worried they might decide to expel you this time?"

"Not really. Quentin will smooth things over—they'll listen to him; he gives them lots of money." He gave the whole matter a dismissive wave. "I don't really care, one way or the other. I've had enough of school."

Izzy gave that a rare smile. "I'm not crazy about school, either, to be honest. My parents, though..." She trailed off, the smile fading. "We should get going."

"All right." The two of them proceeded into a cement stairwell adjacent to Xerxes Avenue, where a small sewer-maintenance entrance had been installed. The steel door at the bottom of the stairwell was locked, but Kaden had acquired a key during a previous adventure.

He pulled the door open. "Stinks," Izzy commented. One of the tendrils of her cloak slithered up to her nose and helpfully pinched it shut for her.

"You didn't expect it to smell *good* down here, did you?" He clicked on a flashlight and peered into the gloom; it was pitch-black inside. "Watch your step," he told her. "There's a steel platform just beyond the door, but it's not very wide."

The steel platform was situated at the top of a vertical shaft, about thirty feet deep; at the bottom of this shaft was a long, seemingly endless brick-walled corridor which branched off into several other corridors. Signal City's sewer system, a vast underground world of man-made caves and tunnels, spread out from here.

They passed through the steel door and descended into the corridor by way of a rusty, creaking old ladder. "Which way?" Izzy asked.

"The Eyeball has two or three hideouts down here," Kaden said, considering, "but his workshop is somewhere underneath the Church of St. Andrew, over on Syracuse Street. It's a bit of a walk, but unfortunately there aren't any other good ways to get there."

"Do you think we'll find him there tonight?"

"Probably. He lives down here, you know."

"He does?"

"Yeah. He's pretty weird."

They began making their way deeper into the sewers. Kaden led the way, his flashlight beam cutting into the darkness. He had a pretty good idea of where he was going, but he *did* have to stop every few minutes to get his bearings.

It wasn't a pleasant stroll by any means. The stench was awful, and there was garbage everywhere. The tunnels were coated with slime and grime, and a muddy, unspeakable muck, several inches deep, flowed sluggishly through them (fortunately, both Kaden and Izzy had remembered to wear their rubber boots, which sloshed with every step they took).

"Hard to believe anybody could live down here," Izzy commented, wrinkling her nose as they passed through a particularly malodorous tunnel.

"The Eyeball's shop is actually pretty cozy," Kaden said. "Zona'na gave him some Neptunian tech a while back; it keeps the damp out, somehow, and freshens the air."

"Zona'na? That exiled Neptunian prince?"

"Yeah. He lives down here, too. Quarterstaff's worked with him a few times. These sewer-heroes can be a little weird, but they're usually pretty good at what they do. We take a right here."

They turned off into a much more spacious (and much less pungent) tunnel. After several minutes of silence, Izzy asked, "How did you come to be Quarterstaff's sidekick?"

He gave her a backwards glance. "Accidentally."

"Accidentally?"

"I ran away from the Academy when I was fourteen. I didn't

have anybody, and I was in kind of a bad place." *Slashed and bleeding, and looking into a raging storm.* "Quentin...found me. Offered to take me in. The sidekick stuff came later; it was almost two years before he let me join him. Told me I needed to fill out a bit." He rolled his eyes. "But I had the skills from the beginning. He saw that right away."

"I see."

"Why do you ask?"

"I don't know. Just curious, I guess. I know I'm supposed to be a superhero, but I don't actually know a whole lot about them, or about what makes them tick. You're the first one I've met, you know."

"Well, you're about to meet your second. The Eyeball's shop is right around the corner."

Together, the two of them climbed out of the spacious tunnel and into a large underground way station, full of pipes, valves, and rust-brown platforms. There were emergency lights down here, running along the water-stained walls, and they were bright enough to see by; Kaden turned his flashlight off and returned it to his belt.

"This is it?" Izzy asked.

"Not quite. See that big pipe over there? The one that looks like it's been sealed up? That's the entrance to his workshop." He waved her along. "Come on, let's see if he's home."

They picked their way across the chamber—there was trash here, too, and puddles all over the floor—and gave the Eyeball's secret door a couple of knocks.

There was no immediate response. Izzy gave Kaden a questioning look. "How long does it usually take for him to answer the door?" she asked.

He shrugged. "Maybe he's in the shower."

But the steel door unlatched itself (the lock was apparently electronic) and swung open, entirely of its own accord, just a moment later. There was another tunnel beyond this door, but *this* tunnel wasn't anything like a sewer tunnel—it was perfectly sanitary, with perfectly white, porcelain walls. There was florescent lighting on the ceiling, and a welcome mat on the floor.

"Shoes off, please," a faraway voice called out to them, from somewhere inside. The voice echoed through the tunnel.

Kaden pulled his boots off, and after a moment's consideration, Izzy did the same. They proceeded down the tunnel, which was about twenty-five feet long, and emerged into a surprisingly homey chamber, with a spotless cement floor (painted white, and covered over with rugs) and arching brick walls. It wasn't tidy—there was mechanical clutter everywhere—but it was clean; the floor was swept and the walls were dry. It looked vaguely like someone's basement den.

They found the Eyeball sitting at a computer workstation, with his back to them. He was tapping away at a keyboard.

"Good evening," Kaden tried.

"One moment, please," the man said, putting up an index finger. He tapped a few more taps, then, having finally completed whatever it was that he was doing, spun around in his chair to face them. "Skirmish, isn't it? Good to see you! What can I do for you tonight?"

The Eyeball was an odd-looking fellow. He was an older man, very pale, with long gray hair and a funny, elfin face. He had a huge black helmet perched atop his head, and he was wearing a coat that looked something like a bomber jacket, but which was covered in gadgetry; he had circuit boards built into his shoulders (they looked like epaulettes) and blue cables snaking all around his arms and into a pair of wired-up gloves.

A single, huge magnifying glass, attached to his helmet by a spindly metal arm, was positioned in front of his right eye. The glass —part of a homemade, head-mounted display—made the eye look gigantic; Kaden could see the blood vessels in his sclera. The hero's penchant for wearing this strange device had, of course, earned him his unusual *nom de guerre*.

Before Kaden could reply, the Eyeball's giant, magnified eye fixed itself on Izzy. "I don't think we've met." He rose to his feet. "My name's Phinneas. They call me the Eyeball."

She shook his gloved hand. "I'm the White Ribbon," Izzy said. "It's nice to meet you."

"That's an interesting cape you have there. Magic?"

"Yes."

He made a disapproving noise. "Not a fan of magic myself. No offense! I've just never been able to make sense of the rules. Math is a *lot* simpler." He swung his eyeball back to Kaden. "Quarterstaff's not with you?"

"No. He's overseas, training Garnet for something."

"Ah. I've been meaning to thank him for the help he gave me on that Rat Fink case; perhaps you could send him my regards. Excellent fellow! One of the best of us."

"Uhh...right."

"So what did you want to see me about?"

"I have some questions," Izzy said. "Are you...busy?"

He shook his helmeted head. "Quiet night. I was just heading out to replace a security camera at the Falcon Tunnel Intersection—the Minotaur's labyrinth materializes in that area once in a while, and I like to keep ahead of it. But it can wait!"

"Oh. Okay." She looked at Kaden, looked back at the Eyeball, then said, "I understand you spoke with Joe Arroyo shortly before he was murdered."

His face fell a bit. "Arroyo. Yes. He sought me out. An awful tragedy, what happened to him; he was a very dedicated detective. The fact that he ventured down *here*, to see *me*, speaks for itself; not many SCPD detectives would've done that. Are you investigating his murder?"

"Sort of. What did he want to talk to you about?"

Eyling scratched his head. "He told me he was investigating the disappearance of a young lady. He wanted to know if–"

"A young lady?" Izzy asked excitedly. "Olivia Pottinger?"

"No...no, that wasn't the name." He stopped to think for a moment. "The girl's name was Mariana, I believe. Nine years old. You'll have to forgive me; I can't seem to remember her surname."

Izzy looked confused. "Mariana?"

He nodded. "The girl went missing a few months ago, apparently. Detective Arroyo wanted to know if the security camera I had installed at the Duncan Outfall had captured anything unusual on the night she disappeared. She was last seen around Cincinnatus Park, you see, which isn't far from the Outfall—in fact it sits below it, on a cliff overlooking the sea."

She frowned at all that. "Did your camera record anything interesting, then?"

"I'm afraid not. That camera only covers a very small portion of the northern side of the park, and only from a great distance. But it was a fine idea, certainly! Worth investigating. I don't think anyone else in the SCPD would've even considered the possibility."

Kaden glanced at Izzy. "I take it you hadn't heard about this Mariana going missing."

"No."

"Are the two of you looking into this recent spate of disappearances, then?" Eyling asked.

Kaden raised an eyebrow. "Disappearances? Plural?"

"Oh, yes. Arroyo was investigating several of these cases—at least, that's what he told me. Over the past five months at least ten children have gone missing in Stone's Row."

"*Ten?*"

"At least."

"Why haven't we heard about this on the news?" Izzy wondered. "Ten children going missing, over such a short period of time..."

The Eyeball shook his head sadly. "Alas. According to Arroyo, these children all had something in common. They were...let's call them *disadvantaged*. Runaways, foster kids, the products of badly broken homes..." He shrugged. "They fell through the cracks, one by one, and...well, nobody noticed, until Arroyo spotted the trend."

"He believed these disappearances were connected?" Kaden asked.

The older man nodded. "Indeed. The SCPD remains unconvinced, apparently, but Arroyo was sure he was on to something...and personally, I think he was, too. Alarming!"

"Olivia was a runaway," Izzy mused. "Sort of. I wouldn't call her disadvantaged, though, not by a long shot." She turned to the Eyeball. "Is it just girls who are disappearing?"

"No, no. More boys than girls, actually."

"How old?"

"That seems to vary. I believe Arroyo said the average age was eleven or twelve."

"So we're not just dealing with a single kidnapping here," Izzy said, the excitement in her voice returning. "We're dealing with *multiple* disappearances. This is...this is good news."

Kaden blinked. "It is?"

"Well, it's not *good* news, obviously, but...don't you see? If these cases are all connected, then solving any of them might lead us to Olivia. We've got leads now that we didn't have before."

"I suppose that's one way of looking at it." He gave the Eyeball a polite nod. "Thanks for your help. I'll be sure to give Quarterstaff your...regards, when he gets back."

"Yes, excellent. But you're leaving already? I have some

refreshments here..." He started rummaging through a cabinet.

"That's okay," Kaden said quickly. He wasn't really keen on the idea of imbibing anything down here. "We should get going."

"Which way are you headed? Perhaps you'd like to accompany me to the Falcon Tunnel Intersection—it's pretty lively down there, especially at this time of night."

"No, thanks. Like I said, we should probably get going; we've got our work cut out for us, I think, on these kidnapping cases."

Eyling nodded, in a resigned sort of way. "I understand. Well, good luck to you! I hope the two of you can solve this mystery...but don't forget what happened to that poor detective." He wagged a bony finger at them. "Keep your eyes open—both of them!"

"We will," Izzy said. "And thanks again."

Pulling on their boots, they left the Eyeball's hideout and began making their way through the muck, back to the maintenance entrance behind the Barnes Theater.

"That was productive," Kaden volunteered.

"Yeah," Izzy said distractedly.

He glanced at her. "Something the matter?"

"What? Oh, no, nothing's the matter. I was just thinking."

"About what? These disappearances?"

"Among other things." She threw a backwards glance down the tunnel. "I got the impression that the Eyeball didn't really want us to leave."

"He's probably lonely," Kaden agreed. "He's lived down here for almost thirty years, you know, and he's been alone for most of that time."

"He's not the only superhero who lives down here, though, is he?"

"Oh, no, not at all. Carcass has a base in Olympia, and Zona'na lives over by Gateway East. Pretty Penny probably has a headquarters down here, too, somewhere. But I don't think these sewer-heroes are inviting each other over for tea very often; they tend to be pretty antisocial. Heck, you can't even carry on a conversation with Pretty Penny—she's *constantly* talking to herself." He shrugged. "It's not like he never has any visitors—lots of heroes drop by to consult with him, like we just did—but anyone would get lonely after a few years of living down here in this dank."

"I feel bad for him," she said quietly, her eyes downcast.

Izzy clearly identified with Eyling's loneliness. Kaden gave her a brief, thoughtful look, then asked, "Do you have any brothers or sisters, Izzy?"

She shook her head. "I'm an only child."

"Me, too. Where'd you grow up?"

"All over," she replied, starting to sound a little puzzled. "My family has several houses, all over the country; we were always moving around."

"I moved around a lot when I was a kid, too. My uncle was always switching apartments, and the Academy was always moving, to avoid the cops; we never stayed in one place for very long. Where'd you go to school, before you transferred to Jeffries?"

She stopped walking. "What's with all these questions?"

"Humor me."

She sighed. "I had a tutor when I was little. I started going to actual schools when I was about thirteen—I was at Enterprise for a year, and then Wallace Prep, and Elkins-Courier..."

"That's quite a few."

"My parents' fault. They kept moving me around, because..."

"Because?"

"Because I never really fit in anywhere, and...and they *wanted* me to fit in. They still do." She shook her head, disgusted.

"Hard to make friends when you're moving around so much," Kaden said. He was beginning to understand her a little better, he thought. She tried to hide it under a cool, unflappable exterior, but Izzy was, in her own way, just as lonely, just as isolated, as the Eyeball.

He sympathized. He'd had some of the same problems, growing up.

"I suppose," she admitted. But then her voice turned icy. "I don't need your pity, you know."

He spread his hands. "I didn't mean to offend you. I was just making an observation."

She gave that a skeptical snort, but said nothing in reply.

They climbed out of the sewers a few minutes later, reemerging in the narrow alley behind the theater. "Thanks for your help," Izzy said curtly.

"You're welcome. Keep me appraised, okay? If there's anything else I can do—"

"I'll let you know." She turned to leave...but then stopped, and turned to face him again. "I'm sorry."

"About what?"

She looked a little flustered. "I'm new at this, okay? I don't always say the right thing, or *do* the right thing. This stuff isn't...it's not *easy* for me."

Kaden frowned. "Nobody ever learned to be a superhero overnight–"

"I wasn't talking about that." But before he could ask her what she meant, her tangled cloak ejected a pair of ribbons into the sky and dragged her lithe form out of the alley.

CHAPTER EIGHT

Quentin called him the next day. "We're taking a break from the training," he said. "We're in Carmarthen right now, waiting for Cadwaladr to show up. Weather's terrible. What's been happening in Signal City?"

Kaden told him he'd been suspended from school.

He groaned. "I told your principal this wouldn't happen again," he complained. "I gave her my word."

"Sorry, boss."

"This is really going to cost me, kid. You know that, right?" He groaned again. "You couldn't have just walked away?"

"Sure, but he would've kept after me. The guy wanted a fight...so I gave him one."

He sighed. "I assume you won?"

"Naturally."

"What were the damages?"

"Broke his nose."

"Aww, jeez, kid."

"Sorry, boss."

"All right, all right. I've had enough of this subject. I'll do what I can to get you back in there, but you're gonna have to work with me, okay? No more of this fighting in school. Save it for the streets."

"Right." He didn't think anyone else at Jeffries would be stupid enough to challenge him anyway, after what he did to Russell.

"Speaking of the streets...have you had any luck finding those stolen swords?"

"Not really. The truth is, I've been caught up in another mystery lately." And he proceeded to give Quentin a rundown of all that had happened since he'd left the country: he told him about his visit to Joe Arroyo's apartment, and of how he'd encountered Izzy afterward and gotten caught up in her missing persons case.

"Sloppy work," Quentin said. "Allowing the girl to discover your secret identity. I suppose she figured out mine as well?"

"I'm afraid so."

"Damn. Well, it can't be helped. Can we trust her?"

"I think so. She can be a little...*strange*, sometimes, but I'm getting along with her okay now, and I don't think she has any interest in exposing us."

"Good." He chuckled. "Isidora Rushforth, huh? Who would've thought?"

"Do you know her?"

"No, but I've met her father a few times; he's a Daniels Corporation shareholder. Serious guy. All business."

"What about these Pottingers? You know anything about them?"

"Not really. I'd heard about their daughter's disappearance, of course, but I didn't dig into it; it looked like a pretty straightforward murder case to me. You're telling me there's been multiple kidnappings, and that Arroyo believed there was some kind of connection between them?"

"That's right."

"Huh. Interesting."

"Any theories?"

"Nothing's coming to mind. The Night Terrors used to abduct children, to turn them into Renfields, but the Terrors aren't around anymore—they disbanded after Miracle Girl threw Cane into the Demonic Realm. And I seem to recall the Red Masque tried pulling a Pied Piper scheme a few years ago, but...no, that's no good. The Masque's in prison, and anyway he makes it a point never to repeat a performance." He paused for a moment, evidently thinking the matter over. "I don't think we have enough to go on at this point."

"We could be dealing with an ordinary serial killer," Kaden suggested.

"That's possible, too. Keep me informed, eh?"

"Yeah." He took a deep breath here, before continuing; he wasn't exactly looking forward to telling Quentin about this last bit of news. "There's one more thing," he said. "I talked to Sly the other day. You remember him, right? He was one of my instructors at the Academy."

"I remember your mentioning him," he said warily. "What did he want?"

"He wanted to warn me....about Rio. He's back in Signal City."

"Rio," Quentin said, with obvious distaste. "I don't like *this* news. What's he been up to?"

"The Dark's been assigning him assassinations. In fact he might've been the one who killed Detective Arroyo."

Quentin swore. "I don't like this. I don't like this at all."

"I'm not too thrilled about it, either."

"I suppose you're thinking about going after him."

"Well, yes, actually..."

"That's not a good idea," he said flatly.

"Why not? The guy's *dangerous*. He's been killing people for the Dark, and he's almost certainly planning on coming after *me*, too. Sly said as much. If I can get the drop on him—"

"Not a good idea," Quentin repeated.

"He might even be the one who's been going around stealing these mystical weapons for Sho Matsumoto," Kaden continued. "I'm not going to ignore the guy, and what he's doing, just because I have a history with him."

"I just don't want you doing anything stupid, kid. I don't want you doing anything...reckless."

Kaden knew what he was implying. "You're afraid I'll kill him."

"I'm afraid," Quentin said carefully, "that in the heat of the moment, you might do something you'll regret. I was *there* the last time, Kaden. Remember? I saw the fight; I saw the look in your eyes. I *don't* want to see that look again."

"That was a long time ago," he said sullenly. "Things are different now."

"I hope so," he sighed. "Here's the question you need to ask yourself, Kaden: are you aiming to go after Rio because you want to get to the bottom of this case, and stop these assassinations...or because you feel like you've got a score to settle with the guy?"

"I..." He frowned, thinking about it. "It's a bit of both."

"That's what I thought. And *that's* why I'm worried."

"Quentin..."

"I've gotta go, kid. Think about what I said, okay? And don't...don't do anything stupid."

"No promises," Kaden muttered.

* * *

The conversation left Kaden in a bad, sulky mood. He understood that Quentin was just looking out for him, but the fact that his mentor didn't *trust* him—at least where Rio was concerned—was disappointing, and a little irritating as well. Quentin, it seemed, still saw him as that troubled, fourteen-year-old kid from the Academy—the kid he'd found on that rain-slicked rooftop, covered in blood and clutching a sword. The kid who had fallen, sobbing, into his arms.

It bothered him.

To raise his spirits, he decided to go out that night, as Skirmish. Climbing on his motorcycle, he roared out of the parking garage and headed south—maybe, he thought idly, he could find some worthwhile action down in Concord, or across the bridge in Lowtown.

He had a police scanner built into his motorcycle helmet, and he switched it on, out of habit, as he began making his way across the surface streets. There didn't seem to be a whole lot going on in the city, apart from a few carjackings and domestic disturbances, but around eleven-thirty he caught something on the scanner that pricked up his ears: a reported theft at the Nordic Heritage Museum on Princip Boulevard, down in Wellington.

Kaden had heard of that museum. A few months ago, the time-tossed Northmen—a bloodthirsty crew of Viking pirates, led by a brute called Bloodbane—had attacked the Dreamworld amusement park on King Island, just north of the city. Kaden, along with Quentin, Shieldmaiden, and a few other heroes, had eventually managed to drive them back to their ship...but the pirates had left a number of their ancient, enchanted weapons behind, and Shieldmaiden, he recalled, had made a point of donating some of them to that Nordic Heritage Museum.

Maybe it was just a coincidence, but to Kaden this reported robbery smelled like another possible weapons theft. And since Princip Boulevard was nearby, he decided to check it out.

Wellington was a sprawling, upscale neighborhood, with a vaguely suburban feel to it; it was full of trees and parks. The museum, housed in an old, historic mansion, was situated on the northeastern side of the neighborhood, near the coast, at the end of a leafy cul-de-sac; Kaden parked his motorcycle a couple of blocks away and, sticking to the shadows, quietly approached the building.

There were two police cruisers parked in front of the museum, both with their lights on. A couple of officers were chatting with a middle-aged woman out front; evidently she was explaining the circumstances of the burglary to them.

There was a nicely-landscaped area, complete with a gazebo and a large, shady grove of trees, on the eastern side of the mansion, not far from where the officers were speaking to the woman. Kaden, hoping to overhear something, crept into this grove, but he was still too far away to make out what the middle-aged woman was saying. He decided to wait until the cops left, and then try speaking to the woman himself to find out what had happened.

He was waiting there, patiently, when he suddenly got the feeling that he wasn't alone. He glanced to his right...and, out of the corner of his eye, saw a dark figure emerge from behind a tree, about twenty feet away from where he stood. The figure immediately bolted, disappearing further into the grove.

Kaden didn't know who this dark figure might be, but the fact that they were skulking around the museum was obviously suspicious, and he decided on a pursuit. Running hard, weaving his way through the trees, he chased the figure all the way out of the grove and up to a high wooden fence—the property line, he assumed. His quarry found a couple of footholds and vaulted over the fence easily; Kaden, a second or two later, did the same.

But by the time he'd landed on the other side, the shadowy figure had already disappeared.

Puzzled, and a little annoyed at having lost the skulker so quickly, he looked around...and got lucky, *just* spotting the figure as he ran across a street and into a dimly-lit parking lot.

Kaden again gave chase, crossing the street and pursuing the figure through the parking lot and into an adjoining baseball stadium.

It was a small stadium—probably it was used by the local high school or something—and the two of them entered it on the dugout side, climbing over a chain-link fence and entering a concrete complex beneath the stands, where some locker rooms and bathrooms had been installed.

Kaden chased the figure through this complex and out onto the field, only to find that, once again, the mystery man had somehow managed to elude him. Cautiously, he took a few steps onto the grass, scanning the dark ball field for any sign of movement. Where had the figure gone?

He was considering returning to the stands—maybe the man had doubled back, into the complex?—when, out of nowhere, a knife suddenly shot out of the darkness. He dodged it by sheer luck, catching a glint of it as it flashed by his face and throwing his head back just in time to avoid it.

"Oh, come on, dude," a sarcastic voice called out to him. "How could you miss that one? It was right over the plate!"

Kaden started. He *knew* that voice. He hadn't heard it in three years, but...

Rio Killian was sitting on top of one of the dugouts, his legs dangling over the side. He was masked, and, like Kaden, dressed all in black. His old rival was lean and muscular, about six feet tall, with predatory eyes and a shock of yellow-blond hair. A pair of Chinese butterfly swords—his signature weapon—hung from his belt, but he had other weapons as well; Kaden could see a collapsible baton attached to one of his forearms and a brace of throwing knives thrown over his chest.

Kaden clenched his fists. "Rio," he growled.

"Do I know you?" He leaned forward a bit, peering down at him. "Wait a minute...Kaden? Is that you?" He sounded genuinely surprised.

"It's been a while."

"Well, I'll be damned. It *is* you." He jumped off the dugout, kicking up a cloud of dust as he landed in the dirt. "This saves me some trouble. I've been looking for you, you know."

"Yeah, I heard."

Rio grinned. It was a very charming grin; Rio had always been a charming guy. "Kaden. Boy, seeing you sure brings back some things." He began making his way over to him, his movements panther-like. "How've you been?"

"What were you doing back there, Rio? Slitting throats?"

The assassin shook his head sadly. "Oh, come on, Kaden. Is that any way to talk to an old friend? We haven't seen each other in three years—"

"We're *not* friends."

His eyes narrowed. "We used to be. And if you hadn't left the Academy, hadn't spit in our faces like you did, we'd *still* be friends."

"That's debatable."

"We were your *family*, Kaden. You *betrayed* us."

"What were you doing at that museum?"

He scowled at the change of subject. "Would you believe I've recently acquired an interest in Scandinavian history?"

"You broke in," he said. "You stole the Northmen's swords, the swords Shieldmaiden donated to the place."

"Do I look like I'm carrying any swords?" He slid his butterfly blades out of their scabbards and twirled them around in his hands. "Apart from these, I mean?"

"Obviously you stashed them somewhere—maybe in that grove of trees I chased you out of."

"Please." He took another couple of steps forward—slowly, menacingly.

"What's this all about, Rio? Why are you chasing after all these strange weapons?"

"Weapons?" Kaden thought he detected a bit of calculation in his voice.

"Don't play dumb. The Dark's been running around the city, stealing these enchanted artifacts, for months now—and last week you murdered Joe Arroyo, probably because he knew too much about it."

"Arroyo?" He rolled the name around on his tongue. "Never heard of the guy."

"You're lying."

"And *you're* starting to piss me off," he said impatiently. He gave his blades another couple of twirls. "Accusing the Dark of these thefts to justify this vendetta of yours..." He shook his head angrily. "That's what this is all about, isn't it? We haven't stolen anything. You know that as well as I do."

Vendetta? What was *this* about?

"You're a traitor, Kaden. Worse than a traitor. What have you done with the Satsujinken?"

Kaden frowned. "What the hell are you talking about?"

"You know damn well what I'm talking about."

"No, I don't."

He snarled at that. The charm had disappeared; he was all rage now. Typical Rio. "Fine," he spat. "I'm sick of talking anyway. I haven't forgotten, you know—I've been waiting for this for three years. *Three years.*" He pointed at Kaden's tonfa with one of his swords. "Get 'em out."

Kaden took a deep breath, drew his tonfa, and fell into a fighting stance—the *neko-ashi-dachi*. Rio did the same, though his stance was much looser, much more relaxed.

Just like old times.

Rio feinted a few times, to get a sense of his speed, and then attacked: transferring both swords into one hand, he slashed downwards, then tossed one of the blades into his free hand on the upstroke and came at Kaden fast, carving up the air in front of him like some kind of crazed butcher. Kaden blocked a few slashes with his tonfa, but didn't fully engage him; those blades were flying at him too damn fast. He *hated* butterfly swords. No room for error.

So he backpedaled, catching a blow here and there, but mainly just doing what he could to defend himself. The last time they'd fought, Rio had worn himself out, swinging those heavy swords around, after which Kaden had turned the tide with his own offensive; he figured the same strategy would work a second time.

Unfortunately, Rio didn't seem to be running out of gas—those swords of his were still slashing, as fast as ever, three or four minutes later, and it was Kaden who was having trouble keeping up.

The fight was taking them into the infield, between second and third base. Batting one of the swords away as it sliced at him—too close for comfort—he spun around, pushed his way past Rio's guard, and performed an *ushiro-hijiate*, jamming his tonfa into his rival's abdomen before rolling away to gain a bit of distance.

The blow didn't bother Rio all that much—he was probably wearing some kind of body armor—but it backed him off, which gave Kaden a little time to think.

Rio was taller than him, by several inches, and weighed quite a bit more. He was stronger than he'd been three years ago; there was much more power behind his swings, and his reach seemed a bit longer now, too. And he was *fast*, faster than Kaden remembered.

He smiled wolfishly, despite himself. *This*, at least, was a real fight.

Rio came at him again, this time holding the swords in a reverse grip, similar to the way Kaden held his tonfa. Kaden countered this by flipping his tonfa around—holding them by their shafts, in a *tokushu* grip—and blocking the blades as they slashed up at him. Before he could hook the swords out of Rio's hands, however—the obvious tactic here—the assassin effortlessly returned to a standard grip and started slicing into him again, pushing him back once more. His assault was just as furious as ever.

Kaden was breathing hard by now...and Rio didn't seem to be. He was doing things Kaden had never seen him do before, pulling off complicated sword-tricks with a few flicks of his wrist. His footwork was good; his countering was excellent.

He'd improved.

Kaden grimaced. His rope-a-dope strategy wasn't working, and he didn't think he could hold Rio off much longer. It was risky, but if he was going to survive this, he was going to have to get in there and *fight*, before the other man's onslaught tired him out.

Resolved, he threw himself at his old friend, countering his sword-swings and trying to hit him with a variety of different blows: he aimed high, with *shuto-uchi* strikes; he tried for his midsection; and at one point he even tried a leg sweep. He paid for this last; Rio caught him as he was jumping away, slashing at his left forearm. It wasn't a deep or serious wound, but it stung. Kaden grunted in frustration.

"What's the matter?" Rio drawled. "You sick or something? You're holding back."

Kaden didn't reply to that; instead, he renewed his attack, swatting away Rio's blades (both of his tonfa were pretty beat up by now) and trying to bully his way in close again. Finally spotting an opening, he ducked low, barely avoiding the blades as they cut through the air over his head, and slammed a tonfa into Rio's knee. He stumbled away, but managed to bring one of his swords down as he fell back; Kaden, fortunately, saw it coming, and was able to block it. The two of them parted.

"Better," Rio grunted. He started flexing his leg a little, testing the pain—the blow had obviously hurt him. "But you're still holding back. You're not fighting like you used to; you're not trying to *hurt* me. You can't beat me like this."

"You want me to hurt you?" Kaden growled. "I'll hurt you."

Rio smirked. "I don't think you can. You've gone soft, Kaden."

Angry now, and still desperate to end this fight before his stamina failed him, Kaden rushed the smirking bastard—which proved to be a singular mistake. As he charged ahead, Rio tossed one of his butterfly swords straight up into the air—to draw Kaden's eye —and then pulled a throwing knife out of his belt and flung it at him. Kaden spotted it at the last second and tried to throw himself out of its way, but he wasn't fast enough; the blade, about five inches long, embedded itself in his right shoulder, just above his breastplate. The knife only went in about an inch and a half, but it shocked him. Distracted by the impact, and the pain, his attack faltered, and Rio followed up the throw by bum-rushing him so fast that Kaden tripped over his own feet and fell backwards onto the grass. His tonfa went flying.

Rio, looking down at him, snorted in derision. "Three years," he said, his voice icy, "and *this* is all I get?" He drew another knife from his belt.

Kaden was already reaching for his own belt, though. He hated to resort to this, but he didn't have much of a choice at this point.

His rival raised the knife...and Kaden grabbed for his dart gun. Pressing the button to flip the barrel out, he cocked it by slapping the bottom of the grip and aimed it up at Rio, his finger on the trigger.

Rio stopped in mid-throw, and the two of them, caught in this stand-off, looked into each other's eyes.

"Pathetic," Rio said, spitting the word out like a curse.

"This isn't a toy," Kaden warned him. "At this range, the bolt in this thing will go right through you." Which wasn't *exactly* true; the dart he'd just loaded probably wouldn't even penetrate Rio's armor. A shot to his unprotected neck, or face, however, would certainly leave him gravely injured.

"I'm disappointed in you, Kaden," the assassin sighed, backing off a few steps. "What happened to the kid I fought three years ago? The kid who almost killed me with my own sword?"

Kaden kept him in his sights, saying nothing.

"I was hoping to put an end to this tonight, but if this is how you want to play it..." He lowered his knife. "Fine. See you around." And he sprinted off, into the deep darkness of the outfield. Kaden watched him disappear.

The encounter hadn't gone anything like he'd expected. The dart gun had kept Rio from carrying out the *coup de grace*, but there was no question he'd won the fight. He'd gotten better, over the past three years—considerably better. He'd obviously been devoting himself to his training.

I've fallen behind.

Angry, frustrated, and, if he was being truthful, more than a little humiliated, he threw the dart gun to the ground, yanked the knife out of his shoulder (ignoring the blood and the pain) and began stalking his way back to where he'd stashed his motorcycle.

Rematch. Rematch.

CHAPTER NINE

*H*e found a doctor to stitch him up—Quentin's usual guy, who tended not to ask any questions—and spent the following day, Sunday, pacing around his penthouse. He was in a foul mood; he wanted to beat someone up, or at least blow off some steam with some weight training, but his shoulder ached, and the doctor had warned him not to aggravate it. So he stewed, in his apartment, stomping through his rooms and scowling at the rain, which was falling hard outside his window.

Rematch. Rematch.

Finally, bored and restless, he took his shirt off, hopped on his treadmill, and started running, hard. His shoulder throbbed, but he ignored it; he was too angry at himself to care.

Late in the afternoon, a call came up from the lobby—he had a visitor. Turning off the treadmill, he toweled himself off, keyed up the elevator, and went over to the foyer.

It was Izzy who stepped off the elevator. She was wearing casual clothes, and Kaden—who had only ever seen her wearing her school uniform or her White Ribbon costume—was a little surprised to see how different she looked in them. The fashionable jacket and jeans softened her a bit, made her look a bit more...well, *ordinary* wasn't exactly the right word, but it was close.

Izzy was even more surprised to see *him*, though—her blue eyes bugged out when she saw that he wasn't wearing a shirt.

"H-hi," she said uncertainly. "Are you busy, or...?" She seemed to be having a hard time taking her eyes off his muscled torso.

"No," he said. "Come on in."

"What happened to your shoulder?"

"Got in a fight," he grunted. "What's up?"

The two of them walked into his spartan living quarters. She gave the room a top-to-bottom look. "No frills, huh?"

He shrugged. "It's not my house. It's Quentin's."

"Is he back in Signal City yet?"

"No. Still in Wales." He found a shirt and threw it on, wincing as he moved his shoulder. "What's going on, Izzy? What are you doing here?"

"I just wanted to know if you'll be back in school tomorrow. If you're not gonna be around, they'll probably make me find a new partner for that history presentation."

"Is that all? You didn't have to come all the way down here to ask me that."

"Actually, I did. I don't have your number."

He blinked. "Oh. Here, I'll give it to you. Just let me find my phone..." He found the phone and gave her the number, which she added to her contact list.

"So are you going to school tomorrow or not?"

"I guess so," he grouched. "I got a text from Quentin this morning. He got me off the hook, somehow."

"Oh. Good."

"What's good about it?" He went over to the window and looked out at the rain. "School..." He shook his head dismissively. "Waste of time. I wish they *had* expelled me." And then he growled something inarticulate.

She looked at him curiously. "Is something wrong?"

"I'm in a bad mood."

"Yeah, *obviously*. But why? What happened to your shoulder?"

"I told you. I got in a fight."

Her eyes narrowed suspiciously. "With who?"

"No one you know."

"A supervillain?"

"Not exactly."

She frowned. "You don't want to talk about it?"

"No," he said brusquely. "I don't."

"Oh." She stood there awkwardly for a moment, then said, "Sorry. I guess it's really none of my business, is it?" There was a hint of sadness in her voice. "All right, then. See you tomorrow, Kaden."

He gave her a considering look, as she began making her way back to the elevator. Izzy could be difficult, and mercurial...but did he really want to push her away like this, just when they were starting to get to know one another?

He realized, quite suddenly, that he didn't.

"Rio," he muttered.

She stopped, glancing back at him over her shoulder. "Rio?"

"Rio Killian." He turned his gaze back to the window. "A friend of mine—well, he *was* a friend—from the Academy. I ran into him last night."

"And you fought."

"Yeah. And he beat me." He touched his wounded shoulder. "He works for the Dark now; he's one of their assassins. There's a good chance he was the one who killed Detective Arroyo."

"Really?"

He nodded. "It's the sort of work he does now, for the syndicate. He wouldn't admit to killing Arroyo, but it's always been hard to pin Rio down on anything. He's *slippery*."

She studied him carefully. "This guy was...your friend?"

"My *best* friend. We grew up together." His eyes fell to the floor. "I left the Academy after my uncle was murdered. He'd worked for the Dark for at least ten years, infiltrating rival syndicates for them, but when he died..." He snorted. "No one cared. I finally realized then that the Academy was rotten—that they were turning me, and all the other students, into tools, and that they didn't really give a damn about any of us. We were all expendable. I'd already become dissatisfied with the place, but after my uncle died...that was it. I left."

He put a pair of fingers up to the window and began tapping absently on the glass. "Remember that big thunderstorm we had on Halloween night, three years ago? That was the night I left. I tried to sneak out without anyone noticing, but Rio found me out, and followed me into the rain." He stopped tapping. "He wanted me to come back—he was screaming at me to come back. Kept going on about family." He laughed bitterly. "I refused. He told me he'd drag me back to the Academy by force, if he had to. I told him to go to hell. That's about when the fight started."

"The fight?"

"The fight. Everything they'd taught us at the Academy—every trick, every counter, every strike... He trailed off, losing himself in the memories. "It was like...it was like the culmination of seven years of training. It was like a final test. Rio and I had always been rivals, really evenly matched, and this fight...it felt like the end of the rivalry. It felt like the end of everything." He gave her an apologetic shrug, when he saw the confused look on her face. "It's hard to explain."

"So what happened?"

"It was a fight. We hit each other, kicked each other, cut each other. We were both bleeding out by the end of it. We'd somehow ended up on a rooftop, soaked to the bone. I'd lost my tonfa, and Rio only had one sword left. I got it away from him, and knocked him down, and..."

"And?"

"And I put the sword to his throat." His face grew troubled. "All I had left then was rage, and I was *raging*. I hated him so much at that moment." He glanced at her. "I almost killed him, Izzy. I came within an *inch* of killing him."

"But you didn't."

"No. Quentin stopped me. He'd seen us fighting on the rooftop, and he showed up there, at the last second, to talk me out of bringing the sword down. But it was *close*." He returned his gaze to the falling rain. "That fight, that *moment*...it did something to me. Messed me up. When you let death get that close..." He trailed off again; he'd never really talked about these things, and words were failing him. "Anyway, it was Rio I fought last night. He put a knife in my shoulder."

Izzy was quiet for a long time. When she finally spoke, it was to ask, "What did Quentin say to you?"

"What?"

"What did he say, to get you to drop the sword?"

"Oh." He smiled slightly at the memory. "He offered to give me a candy bar. Snickers."

She stared. "A candy bar?"

"Yeah. Quentin's like that."

"And that was all it took to convince you?"

"I'd been fighting for my life. I was covered in blood—I've still got the scars from that fight, here and here and here." He pointed out the cuts to her, on his arms and neck. "I was all wrapped up in death, a second away from killing the only real friend I ever had. And then, out of nowhere, this guy in a goofy outfit, wearing a red-and-gold mask, shows up and offers to give me a Snickers bar, if I'll just give him the sword. And he was all casual about it, too, leaning on his staff like he was bored out of his mind." He shrugged. "I guess the absurdity snapped me out of it. I gave him the sword, and Rio got away, and I ended up spending three nights in a hospital getting put back together again." He chuckled. "And he never did give me that damn Snickers bar."

Izzy frowned at him. "Why are you telling me all this?"

"You asked. You wanted to know who I was fighting last night."

"You gave me a lot more than that."

"Am I boring you?"

"No. I'm just...a little surprised, that's all."

In truth, Kaden was a little surprised at himself. Why *had* he opened up to her like that? He hadn't meant to tell her the *whole* story; the words had just sort of tumbled out.

His shoulder was aching. He rotated it a bit, wincing as he did so.

Izzy noticed. "Does it hurt?"

"Yeah, a little. It didn't go in very far, but he got me right in the meaty part of the muscle." He gestured towards his desk. "I kept the knife. It's over there."

She walked over to the desk and picked up the blade, examining it.

Her mouth fell open.

"This? *This* is the knife?"

"Yeah," he said, a little puzzled at this unexpectedly strong reaction. "It's a modified kunai—they call it a whistler. The Dark have been using them for years. Why?"

She looked at him, eyes wide. "This is the same sort of knife they found at the scene of Olivia's kidnapping."

Kaden blinked. "Are you sure?"

"Positive." She looked at the knife intently, turning it over in her hands. "The Dark uses these?"

He nodded slowly. "I trained with them myself, back at the Academy."

"Does anyone else use them?"

"Not that I know of."

She put the knife back down on the desk, but kept her eyes on it. "What does this mean? Is the Dark behind these disappearances?"

"I don't know," Kaden admitted. "The Dark doesn't usually go in for kidnappings, but...I suppose it's possible."

"You spoke with this Rio character last night, right? Did he say anything...suspicious?"

"Not really," he said, thinking back. "It was just the usual taunting. Except..." He frowned. "He accused me of pursuing a vendetta against the Dark, and he mentioned something about the Satsujinken as well. I don't know what he was talking about. He wasn't making much sense."

"The Satsujinken?"

"It's a sword. Belongs to Sho Matsumoto."

"But he didn't say anything about the kidnappings?"

"I didn't think to ask."

Izzy considered that. "I...see." She reached down and picked up the knife again, pressing its tip into her index finger. "You wouldn't happen to know where I can find–"

"No," he said flatly, taking the knife away from her. "You're not going after the Dark."

"Why not?"

"Because they'd kill you."

She crossed her arms. "I'm the White Ribbon."

"You're a teenage girl."

"I have *magic*."

"You wouldn't be the first magician they've killed. They've been around a very, very long time, Izzy; they know how to protect themselves."

"So what are you saying? They're untouchable? We can't investigate them?"

"No. I'm saying we should proceed with *caution*." He set the knife back down on the desk. "We don't want to rush into anything, Miss Rushforth."

That earned him an icy look. "Fine. You know more about the Dark than I do, so...I guess I'll be following your lead on this one."

"Good," he said, relieved.

"But you'll be following *my* lead on this history presentation," she went on, to his dismay, "and you've got work to do. I'll send you some links tonight; we can start putting it all together in the library tomorrow."

"All right, all right," he grumbled. "It's a date."

She gave him a funny look. "It's not a *date*," she said carefully.

He shrugged. "It was just an expression."

She looked a little nonplussed. "Oh."

"You didn't really think—"

"I've gotta go," she said suddenly, hurrying for the foyer. "See you tomorrow, Kaden." And she was into the elevator in about ten seconds flat.

Kaden shook his head, exasperated as usual. *Strange girl.*

He was getting to like her, though.

* * *

He stopped by her locker the next morning, to find out when, exactly, she wanted to visit the library. They set a time, and chatted a bit afterward before heading off to class.

"I saw you talking to that Rushforth girl this morning," Race commented a few hours later, at lunch. "You two have been hanging out a lot lately, huh?"

"We're working on a project together," Kaden said absently. He was in the middle of trying to peel an orange. "History."

"Oh," he said, with an uncharacteristic slyness. "Is that all?"

He looked up at the kid—who, he discovered, was giving him a stupid grin. "What do you mean?"

"Nothing, nothing. It's just...I've been hearing some rumors."

"Rumors?"

"They're saying you beat up Russell Lachmiller last week because he said something bad about Izzy."

"Is that what they're saying?" He snorted derisively. "It was Russell who came after *me*, because I said something bad about Angel."

"Oh. What did you say?"

"I don't remember. I think I called her a cow or something." He popped an orange slice into his mouth. "I *did* beat him up, though—that much is true."

Race looked at him curiously. "Yeah, and how did you manage that, anyway? Russell's not exactly a wimp. He's freaking *huge*."

"Size isn't everything. You ever heard of Jimmy Wilde?"

"No."

"Look him up."

Race shrugged that away. "Well, I hope you can do it again. Word has it he's looking for a rematch."

Kaden sighed. "He's stupider than he looks, then."

"So, about Izzy..." Race pressed.

"I'm *not* going out with her," he said firmly, chewing on another orange slice.

"Oh. Okay." That seemed to be the end of it, but as it turned out Race wasn't *quite* finished with this subject yet. "Hey, maybe you should ask her to the dance."

Kaden stopped chewing. "The dance?"

"Yeah, the week after next. They're having it downtown, in the Lexington 405—top floor, I think. There's some kind of fancy ballroom up there. You know Luke Mahajan, right? The class president? He's the one who offered to hold it there; his family owns the whole building complex. There's going to be a live band and everything."

"School dances aren't really my thing."

"Well, they're not really mine, either, but *I'm* going."

"Oh? Do you have a date?"

"Nah. But I think it'll be fun. You should ask Izzy."

"We're not together, Race. I just told you that."

"You like her, though, don't you?"

Kaden looked at him evenly. "I like a lot of things. I like *oranges*." And he popped another slice into his mouth.

CHAPTER TEN

*T*he following week was uneventful. What Kaden wanted, above all, was that rematch with Rio, but he had no idea where to find his old rival, and his shoulder needed a little time to heal besides, so he spent most of the week taking it easy: exercising, attending school as usual, and working with Izzy on the history presentation. He *did* go out a few times, as Skirmish—he chased down a few muggers, fought a few of the Neo-Rasputin's hippies, and even helped foil a plot to hijack an armored car (the heroine Nightjar did most of the work)—but it was, overall, a pretty dull week.

On Friday, Kaden and Izzy gave their presentation, which went over pretty well (Mr. Kronkenburger seemed to like it, anyway). Unfortunately, Izzy got a bit of stage fright, and Kaden wound up having to do most of the talking.

"Sorry about that," she told him later that afternoon, after classes had ended. "I've never been a very good public speaker."

"You did fine."

"*You* seemed pretty comfortable up there."

He shrugged. "I just imagined everybody naked."

"That doesn't really work, does it?"

He looked her up and down, in a leering sort of way. "It's always worked for *me*."

She tried to slap him; he leaned away from it. "Knock it off," she said crossly.

Kaden chuckled.

The two of them exited the main building, stepping into the shade beneath the cherry trees. "So what's our next step?" Izzy asked him. "In going after the Dark, I mean? Have you settled on a plan of attack yet?"

He shook his head. "I'm still working on it. I'd like to stake out their headquarters, but I don't know where it is; they move the Matsumoto Academy three or four times a year, to throw the authorities off, and they've got safe houses all over. I'm planning on meeting with an old friend tonight, to see if he knows anything; maybe he'll have some clues for us."

"An old friend?"

"His name is Sly. He used to be an instructor at the Academy. He quit the Dark a few years ago, but he still knows some people in the syndicate." He frowned. "Apparently he's into real estate now."

"I see."

"What about you?" Kaden asked. "Did you hit the town last night?"

"Yeah, but I didn't find any real trouble. I heard on the news that the Greenqueen was doing something crazy over in Wellington, so I went down there to check it out, but by the time I arrived the CrossGuard had already taken care of her." She put up a palm. "Stone's Row's been pretty quiet these past few nights...which is a good thing, I suppose. At least there haven't been any more disappearances."

"There haven't been any more thefts, either, to the best of my knowledge. The Dark seems to have gone dark."

"Hmm."

They walked on. After a moment, Izzy turned to him, her expression serious. "Kaden...I have something to ask you."

"What?"

"This...this is going to sound weird."

He raised an eyebrow. "Okaaay..."

"Well, maybe not *weird*, exactly, but coming from *me*..." She was speaking a bit faster now, her words running together. "And I don't want you to take this the wrong way, and I don't want you to think this was *my* idea, and I'd completely understand if you didn't want—"

"Izzy."

She stopped, and sighed. "This stuff isn't easy for me," she muttered.

"It's okay," he said warily. "Just calm down. Take a deep breath." What was *this* all about? And why was she blushing?

"All right." She took the deep breath. "There's a dance next Saturday. I wasn't planning on going, because I *hate* these kinds of things, but my mom found out about it somehow, and..." She hung her head, defeated. "She told me I *have* to go. She told me she'll make my life miserable if I don't."

"Ah." He was beginning to get the picture.

"And," she finished, reluctantly, "she told me I needed to find a date."

"Ah."

"Don't get me wrong," she said quickly, refusing to look him in the eye. "I'm not like, *interested* in you or anything. It's just, you're the only guy I know at Jeffries, and probably the only one who'd understand–"

"I get it," Kaden said. He wasn't all that enthused about the idea of going to a school dance, either, but Izzy seemed pretty stressed out about this, and he didn't mind doing her a favor. "I'll go."

Her head shot up. "You will?"

"Sure. Just so long as you don't get too handsy during the slow numbers. If you try to take advantage of me, I just might–"

"Oh, shut up."

He looked at her curiously. "Why does your mother want you to go to this dance so badly, anyway?"

"It's the same old story," she said, kicking at a pebble. "She wants me to fit in. She wants me to do normal high school things— make friends, go to parties." She shook her head. "It's what she's *always* wanted. She doesn't get me."

"What about your father?"

"Same. He doesn't get me, either."

Kaden frowned. "She said she'll make your life miserable, huh?"

"Yeah. And it wasn't an idle threat; she *knows* how to make my life miserable. She's done it before." Her expression seemed to go blank for a moment. "My parents kind of run my life. They have a lot of...expectations."

"Oh." He didn't know what to say to that. He'd never known his parents, who had died in a car accident shortly after he was born; he found it a little hard to relate.

"Anyway, the dance is Saturday night, at the Lexington 405–"

"Yeah, a friend of mine gave me the details last week."

"Thanks. In advance."

"Forget it. What are friends for?"

* * *

Kaden called Sly shortly after he parted ways with Izzy. "Meet me at my apartment," his old teacher told him. "We can talk there." Sly gave him the address (he lived in Stone's Row, on the second floor of a stately three-story brownstone), and Kaden made his way there later that evening.

Sly's apartment was spacious, and nicely decorated—the walls were full of Japanese woodblock prints, and the wood furniture was all antique. He was obviously doing pretty well for himself.

"How've you been?" Sly asked. "Can I get you something to drink? I've got some Kayo in the fridge. Your favorite, right?"

He smiled. "Right. But I don't want to take up too much of your time, Sly; I just wanted to ask you a few things."

"I've always got time for you, kid." He handed him the bottle of Kayo. "What do you want to know? Is this about the Dark?"

"Yeah," he said, twisting the bottle open. "It's about the Dark. Can you tell me where the Academy's holding classes these days?"

His brow furrowed. "You're still thinking about going after Rio, aren't you? I told you before, I don't think you should be–"

"We've already had our reunion, Sly. I caught him sneaking around the scene of a robbery last week, over in Wellington."

He started. "A robbery?"

"Yeah. More strange weapons."

"So what happened? Did you get into it?"

Kaden pulled his shirt down to show the man his bandaged shoulder. "Yeah. He'd learned a few new tricks, too; I had more trouble with him than usual." And he left it at that; he was too embarrassed to admit that he'd actually *lost* to Rio.

"Ouch. Sorry, kid."

"It's nothing." He shrugged his shirt back into position. "Where's the Academy, Sly?"

He spread his hands. "I don't know."

"You'd tell me if you *did* know, though, wouldn't you?"

80

"Probably not. If you're planning on going after Rio—"

"It's not Rio. It's the Dark." He took a sip of Kayo, swishing the chocolate around in his mouth. "They're up to something, and I'm having a hell of a time figuring out what it is."

Sly regarded him thoughtfully. "Okay. I'm listening."

Kaden pulled Rio's knife out of his pocket and showed it to him. "Recognize this?"

"Sure. It's a whistler."

He nodded. "A knife just like this was found at the scene of a girl's kidnapping back in June."

"Oh?"

"Yeah, and there's been *several* kidnappings in Stone's Row over the past few months. Kids have been disappearing all summer."

Sly frowned. "You think the Dark has been kidnapping *kids?*"

"I think it's possible. Like I said, one of these knives was found at a crime scene. Who else uses whistlers? Fan custom-makes these things in his workshop."

"But why? What's the angle? Ransom?"

"I don't think so. These weren't exactly upper class kids." He paused. "Well, except for one, but she seems to have been the exception."

"I don't know, Kaden," he said doubtfully. "I worked for the syndicate for a lot of years, and I can't remember them ever running a scheme that called for kidnapping little kids."

"You don't think the Dark would sink that low?"

He laughed. "Oh, I *know* they would...but the syndicate is a *syndicate*; they don't care about anything except making money. What would the Dark want with a bunch of brats?"

Kaden made a face. "Good point. Still...I don't know. I've got a funny feeling." He looked up at Sly. "Your contacts haven't mentioned anything about these disappearances?"

"'Fraid not. If Matsumoto *is* behind this thing, whatever it is, he's playing it pretty close to the vest." He poured himself a glass of bourbon, frowning down at the glass. "I *have* heard some rumblings, though, about their next target."

"Another assassination?"

"Yeah. I'm not sure I should give this to you, though. If they send Rio to do the job, and you two get to fighting again—"

"Sly..."

81

He sighed, and paused to take a sip of his bourbon. "The guy's name is Al Muranaka. He's a reporter for the *Sentinel*. He's been digging into the Dark's drug manufacturing business, apparently, and Matsumoto's starting to get *really* sick of him."

"A reporter, huh?"

"Yeah. Must be a pretty dumb one, too. The Dark *hates* publicity." He took another sip. "They're gonna make it look like a home invasion."

"Soon?"

He nodded. "Pretty soon."

"Were you planning on going to the cops with this?"

"The cops can't protect him from the Dark," he snorted. "You know that as well as I do. His best bet is probably to get out of town."

"Yeah, I guess." He finished off his Kayo and set the bottle down. "Thanks for this, Sly."

"The drink, you mean?"

"No, the information."

"So what's your next move? Are you planning on warning Muranaka?"

"Maybe."

His teacher studied him for a long moment. "You're not thinking of using him as bait, are you?"

"Yes, I am, actually. If they send Rio after this guy...maybe I can catch him in the act."

"And then what?"

He smiled grimly. "Rematch."

* * *

It took a bit of prodding, but Sly eventually broke down and provided Kaden with Al Muranaka's address. As it turned out, he lived on the western side of Stone's Row, on Darius Avenue—just a few blocks from the Barnes Theater, from whence Kaden and Izzy had ventured into the sewers the previous week. Muranaka, evidently, was one of the colonizing yuppies Sly had complained about.

His apartment, on the third floor of the Farwell Hotels, sat above a noisy nightclub; people were coming and going constantly. Kaden, using a fake ID to get in, spent the next several nights at the club, blending in with the crowds, in order to surreptitiously observe Muranaka and his movements.

The first thing he learned about the bachelor reporter was that he was hardly ever home—he left his apartment early every morning and rarely arrived home before midnight. This left the Dark with a window of only a few hours, each night, to stage their home invasion; if they wanted to kill Muranaka in his home, as they'd killed Joe Arroyo, they would have to strike during the early morning hours. This made Kaden's job a little easier—it meant he really only needed to stake the place out for a few hours each night—but the hours were inconvenient, to say the least, and he wound up having to skip several days of school.

He was at the Farwell Hotels on Thursday night (actually, Friday morning), watching Muranaka's apartment like usual—the reporter hadn't arrived home yet—when he received a call from Izzy. It was too loud inside the club for him to carry on a phone conversation, so he stepped outside, through a side door, and into a grimy alley.

"Where are you?" Izzy asked, hearing the thundering music over the phone. "What are you doing?"

"Clubbing," he said. He walked around to the front of the building, where he could keep an eye on the front entrance. "What's up?"

"Nothing, I guess. It's just, you haven't been in school for a few days, and I was wondering if we were still on to go to this dance."

"Oh. Yeah. Saturday night, right?"

"Right. It's gonna be kind of a formal thing; I hope you have a tux."

"I'm sure I can find one somewhere."

"So why haven't you been in school lately? You're not sick, are you?"

"That's what I told them, but no, I'm not sick. I've been staking out an apartment building for the past few nights—the Farwell Hotels, on Darius."

"Why?"

He told her what Sly had told him, about Al Muranaka and the murder plot. "So you're protecting this reporter, then?" Izzy asked, after he had finished.

"Well, that's my first priority, obviously," he lied. "But I'm hoping to get my hands on this assassin, too. I'd like to get some information out of him."

She was quiet for a moment. "It's Rio, isn't it? Rio is the assassin they're sending."

"Probably."

"Do you need any help? I can glide down there in a few–"

"I can handle this, Izzy."

"Are you sure? If this guy is half as dangerous as–"

"I can *handle* this," he snapped.

She didn't care for his tone. "Aren't you the one who told me two heads are better than one?"

"This is different. I don't *need* any help, Izzy. I don't *want* any help."

"This isn't about *information*, is it? It's about Rio. It's about *fighting* Rio."

"Of *course* it's about fighting Rio!" he exploded. "It's about–"

But he stopped there, because at that moment, a light suddenly came on in Muranaka's apartment—he could see it through the big, third-floor window above the building's front entrance.

Kaden hadn't seen the reporter enter the building. Who had turned on that light? Who was up there?

"I've gotta go, Izzy," he told her. "Trouble."

"Wait, wait! What's going on? Are you–"

He ended the call there, shoving the phone in his pocket. He then grabbed his tonfa—which he'd stashed in the alley—slipped his mask over his eyes, and entered the building, running up the stairs to the second and then to the third floor.

The door to Muranaka's apartment had been kicked in. Cautiously, Kaden raised his tonfa and stepped into the apartment, pushing the ruined door aside, and looked around.

He couldn't see much. Whoever had turned the lights on had turned them off again, and the interior was dark—much darker than the hallway. Squinting into the pitch-darkness, he found a light switch and flipped it, but nothing happened.

Frowning, he stepped a bit further into the apartment, which was cluttered with books and magazines. He raised his tonfa a bit higher, into a guard; he was beginning to feel very exposed here, and he didn't like it.

"Anyone there?" he called.

No response. Crouching low, and watching the shadows for

signs of movement, he quickly made his way over to the apartment's sole window, the big four-by-four that looked out over Darius Avenue. The shade was half-drawn; he pulled it all the way up, allowing a bit of extra city-light to spill into the main room. The light gave the place an eerie, noirish look.

He looked around, turning his head to the right, to the left, and to the right again, but there didn't appear to be anyone else in the room. Was there someone hiding here, in the bedroom, or the bathroom? He looked around again...

...And that was when a black-clad figure suddenly dropped out of the ceiling, right in front of him, and began slashing at him with a pair of Chinese butterfly swords.

Rio.

Rematch!

Kaden was startled by the man's very sudden appearance, but he'd had his guard up from the moment he'd stepped into the apartment, and he was able to block the first couple of swings. He didn't have a lot of room to maneuver, though—his back was to the wall—and he was having a hard time extricating himself from this furious assault. Rio was really swinging for the fences tonight.

He finally managed to catch one of the blades on an upswing and whirl one of his tonfa into the ninja-masked face of his attacker. The blow missed, but it backed Rio up just a *bit*, allowing Kaden to work his way free of the onslaught. He ended up in the center of the room (much more advantageous), tonfa raised and ready.

Kaden studied his opponent. He was wearing essentially the same outfit as before—a loose-fitting, all-black jumpsuit, with knives slung over his chest and a pair of knee-high shin guards on his legs—but the mask was different; all he could see of his rival's face were his eyes, and these were narrowed into slits.

"If you're looking for Muranaka," Kaden said, "I'm afraid he's not home right now. If you'd like me to leave him a message–"

Rio didn't wait for him to finish—instead, without a word, he threw himself at Kaden again, swords flitting through the air. Kaden recognized several of his techniques, and was able to counter them, but there was a lot of new stuff mixed in there that gave him trouble, and before long he was falling back a second time, unable to do much more than defend himself.

Damn. Damn.

Desperate, he tried a *hirabasami*, and then a figure-eight flip, but Rio seemed to be able to read his mind; he countered every strike with something of his own. The blazing-fast butterfly swords cut into him more than once, slashing into his arms and shoulders; Kaden could feel the blood seeping into the sleeves of his shirt. Rio even managed to cut him once above his left eye, a shallow slice that started the blood flowing immediately. It was only a nick—another fraction of an inch, and it would've been a lot worse—but the blood was blinding him.

Worse, Rio was throwing his heaviest attacks at Kaden's right side, hammering away at his still-healing shoulder. Before long his entire arm was aching.

Frustrated, he lashed out at the bastard, throwing caution to the wind, and managed, at last, to get in a good hit of his own. As Rio stabbed at him, he seized the man's extended arm, wrapped him up, and forced the sword out of his hand. Rio reacted by slashing at him with his free hand, but Kaden knocked the sword away with his tonfa and quickly jammed the butt of his weapon into Rio's gut. As he sucked in a gasp, Kaden gave the assassin's arm—the one he'd wrestled into his grip—a sharp tug, to line it up, and smashed his tonfa into it with all his strength. The blow struck Rio's wrist, and Kaden heard bones cracking.

It was a *very* satisfying sound.

Grunting, Rio yanked his injured arm out of Kaden's grasp. If he was troubled by this turn of events, he didn't show it; he feinted to his right, kicked a coffee table at Kaden, and scooped up his butterfly sword.

And then he continued to fight, one-handed, in an entirely different style.

Kaden had never encountered this particular style of swordsmanship before, and he didn't know how to counter it. Rio was tossing the blade into the air, constantly switching his grip, and coming at him with quick, probing thrusts; Kaden had never seen anyone use a butterfly sword in this manner. The broad blades were made for slashing, not stabbing.

But it was working. He was pressing Kaden back, circling around him, driving him back towards the window. The man was a demon.

It was all Kaden could do to keep that sword at bay. Grunting, he retreated a step...

...And slipped on a pile of magazines. He stumbled back, and Rio took instant advantage: he slapped both of Kaden's tonfa aside with his sword—one, two—pivoted on his left foot, and hit him right in the chest with a roundhouse kick. The force of it threw Kaden into the window, and *out* the window; he smashed through the glass and plummeted into the street below.

Damn.

It was a three-story drop, and he didn't expect to survive it. He tumbled towards the asphalt, shards of glass tinkling all around him, and wondered how it would feel to crash into the street. Would he feel any pain, or would it just be *over*, instantly?

He braced himself...but the life-ending *crash* never came. Instead of landing on the hard, unforgiving street, he landed on something that felt like a big, fluffy pillow. Bits of glass rained down on him; he shielded his eyes from them.

"Got you!" a familiar voice cried.

What the...? Removing his hand from his eyes, he saw that Izzy—Izzy!—had managed to catch him, cushioning his fall by shaping her magical ribbon into a huge hammock. She floated him gently down to the ground, her enormous cloak deflating and shrinking back up into itself as soon as the two of them were safely on the sidewalk. Kaden, returning to his feet, staggered out of the hammock and promptly fell forward, onto his knees. He grimaced.

"Easy, easy," Izzy said, rushing over to him. "Are you okay? God, you're bleeding all over."

"I'm fine," he growled, pulling himself off the ground. "What are you doing here?"

She shrugged. "I thought you needed help."

"You thought wrong."

She regarded him skeptically. "Really? Because from where I'm standing–"

"I didn't *need* any help!" he shouted, whirling on her. "I *told* you I could handle this!"

Her eyes widened at his sudden fury...and then narrowed. "What's *wrong* with you? Who do you think you are, anyway? If I hadn't shown up here just now, you'd be dead. *Dead.*"

He angrily wiped the blood out of his eye. "I need to get back up there. I can't let him get away this time. I can't let him *win* this time."

"You're hurt," she told him.

"I'm *not* hurt. I can still fight." He began stumbling towards the building's front entrance.

"You're *hurt*," she insisted. A series of tendrils suddenly shot out of her cloak, and she began climbing them up to the shattered window on the third floor. "Wait here; *I'll* take care of this Rio character."

"No, no!" He grabbed at one of her ribbons and pulled it back down. "He's mine!"

She looked down at him. "What's gotten into you?" The ribbon he was holding on to slipped out of his grasp, and she proceeded up to the window.

Kaden swore and ran back into the building. He found Izzy waiting for him, in Muranaka's smashed-up apartment; there was no sign of Rio.

"Messy," she commented, throwing back her hood.

Kaden stormed over to the window and retrieved his tonfa. "I'm going after him."

"Where did he go?"

"I don't know," he said, trying to hide the exhaustion in his voice. The fight, followed by another run up two flights of stairs, had left him short of breath. "But he can't have gotten far. I'm going to find him."

"And then what? You think you can beat him like this?"

"Only one way to find out."

"You're crazy."

"Maybe."

"You're going to get yourself killed!" She shook her head, her platinum-blonde hair swishing from side to side. "You're supposed to be a *hero*. This...this is just bloodlust, Kaden."

"A hero?" He snorted. "You think I'm a *hero*? You don't know anything about me, Izzy."

And he left her there, in the apartment, storming off in search of Rio.

CHAPTER ELEVEN

*H*e failed to find his old foe, after two hours of searching, and eventually, inevitably, exhaustion overtook him. He managed to stumble his way over to Quentin's doctor, who treated him once again (most of the cuts Rio had inflicted on him were superficial, fortunately, and only required a few stitches), and afterward made his way back to the Daniels Tower. He took a couple of painkillers, fell into bed, and willed himself to sleep, still angry—angry at Rio, angry at himself, and a little angry at Izzy, too, for coming to his rescue. He hated that she'd had to save him.

His anger at Izzy wasn't really logical, though, and it had faded by the next morning. It wasn't *her* fault, after all, that Rio had kicked him out of that window; he had only himself to blame for that. He'd snapped at her because...well, partly because her interference had annoyed him, but mostly because he'd been embarrassed. He hadn't wanted her to see him like that.

And so, as the sun rose—throwing a warm and golden light into his suite—he decided that he'd better apologize. He called her up.

She didn't answer, but a few minutes later, to his surprise, she showed up at his apartment. "Morning," he said, as she stepped off the elevator.

She skipped the pleasantries. "What happened to you last night? Are you all right?"

"I'm all right," he affirmed. "Rio gave me a few new scars,

but..." He shrugged. "I'll be okay."

"I'm mad at you," she said matter-of-factly.

"Yeah. Look, Izzy, about last night...I'm sorry. I shouldn't have yelled at you like that, especially after what you did for me. I was just..." He shrugged again. "I was a little out of my head."

She raised an eyebrow. "Out of your head?"

He nodded defeatedly. "Rio. It was Rio, again."

"This guy really gets to you, doesn't he?"

"He's improved, over these past three years," Kaden muttered. "*I* haven't. I lost to him again last night, and I took my frustration out on you." He frowned. "I was angry. I was so desperate for that rematch..." He shook his head, disgusted with himself.

She looked at him curiously. "What are you *after*, Kaden? You had your chance to kill Rio three years ago, and you didn't take it. The two of *us* had a chance to capture him, last night, but you insisted on going after him alone." Her eyes narrowed. "So what are you after? If you don't want to kill him, and you don't want to capture him, what exactly do you *want* from this Rio guy?"

"What do I want?" He gritted his teeth. "I want to fight him, and I want to *win*."

"Is fighting—is *winning*—really that important to you?"

"I told you I liked to fight."

"Yes, but—"

"I'm screwed up, Izzy. Okay? I'm screwed up." He closed his eyes and turned away from her. "You're right. You're right about me. I haven't been chasing after Rio to catch him, or because I want to get to the bottom of these cases we've been working on. What I wanted was a *rematch*. I wanted another fight." He slapped his hand against a wall. "I'm not just angry at myself for losing. I'm angry at myself because I'm always...I'm always *fighting*. You called it bloodlust last night; maybe that's what it is. I *enjoy* fighting, for its own sake. I *enjoy* beating up bad guys. And I know I *shouldn't* enjoy it, because superheroes aren't *supposed* to enjoy it, but I do." He sighed deeply. "I'm not like Quentin. I'm not like *you*. I didn't become a superhero because I wanted to use my skills to help people, or for any other righteous reason. If I'm being honest with myself, I...I think I became a superhero because superheroes get to beat people up, and I *like* beating people up." He sighed again. "Rio told me something, that night we fought: he told me I could run away from the Academy, but that I couldn't run away from myself. He was telling me I'd never be anything more than the weapon the Dark had turned me into—that I'd always be a fighter, a killer. I think he may have been right."

"Superheroes *have* to fight sometimes," she said uneasily. "I think you're being too hard on yourself."

He opened his eyes and turned to face her. "Remember, a few weeks ago, when Angel dumped that pudding on your head? I was right there, Izzy. I could've stopped her, but I didn't. I just watched. A *real* hero would've stood up, would've *done* something." He snorted. "Quentin wants me to follow in his footsteps. He wants me to take over for him, after he retires. How can I, though? I'm not a *hero*, Izzy. I'm just a fighter."

She absorbed that. "I understand," she said. "Believe it or not, I understand. And actually, I..." She hesitated, a strange look suddenly crossing her features.

"Yes?"

"I..." She shook her head. "Never mind."

"Anyway," he went on, "I'm sorry. I shouldn't have let Rio get to me, and I shouldn't have taken it out on you."

"Well...okay. Apology accepted." She shrugged. "You were raised by the Dark. I guess I'm not surprised you're a little...maladjusted."

"Thanks," he muttered. "I think."

"So what happened to Rio? I take it you didn't find him?"

"No."

"What about the reporter?"

"He never came home last night."

"Do you think the Dark got to him?"

He shook his head. "I called the *Sentinel* this morning. Apparently he just took a leave of absence. My guess is he got wind of the Dark's plot and decided to book it out of town."

"Oh. Do you think he'll be okay?"

"I don't know. I hope so."

Her eyes suddenly fell on his forehead. "How's that cut over your eye?"

He touched the bandage. "Not bad. Probably won't even leave a scar."

"You're going to have to explain that to my parents, you know."

"I am?"

"You're picking me up at my house tomorrow night, remember? To take me to the dance? My parents want to meet you."

"They do?"

"Unfortunately." She looked at her shoes. "They're making a pretty big deal out of this."

"Oh. Well, I'll try not to disappoint, but..."

"Just be there. Eight o'clock." She turned to leave. "All right. I've gotta get to school. Are you coming?"

"No thanks. Not really in the mood." He gave her a half a smile. "Thanks for coming over, though, and for...listening."

"No trouble," she said. "We're friends. Right?"

"Right," he said. "Friends." But he was looking into her pale-blue eyes as he spoke the words, and was thinking, idly, about how pretty they were.

* * *

The next evening, Kaden cleaned himself up as best he could, had one of Quentin's assistants find him a tuxedo, and made his way down to the private parking garage. He didn't think Izzy would care to be picked up on his motorcycle, so he borrowed one of Quentin's cars instead: an arrest-me red Ferrari 488 (Quentin's preference was for Italian cars). He drove it out of the building and, following the directions Izzy had given him, headed downtown.

The Rushforths were very, very wealthy—right up there with Richard Cross, Victor Vane, and Quentin himself—and they had several homes, on both the east and west coasts. For most of the year, though, they lived on the upper floors of the Madison Building, a grim, obelisk-shaped skyscraper, which also served as the nerve center for the family's business empire. It was a pretty ritzy place.

Kaden left the Ferrari with a valet, and, after dropping by the front desk to give them his name, took the elevator to Izzy's family's suite, on the fifty-seventh floor.

He wasn't really looking forward to this evening, and he especially wasn't looking forward to meeting Izzy's parents. He'd never really *done* anything like this before—picked a girl up for a date—and he didn't know quite what to expect. And the fact that the Rushforths were super-rich only added to his unease. Over the past few years Kaden had rubbed elbows with plenty of rich, upper-class folks, and he knew enough not to make a fool of himself around them, but he had, after all, grown up in a gutter; the bourgeoisie weren't exactly his kind of people.

He was greeted at the elevator by a tall, attractive blonde woman in her forties. The family resemblance being obvious, Kaden took this woman to be Izzy's mother.

"Good evening," she said, extending a hand for him to shake. "You're Kaden, I assume?"

"Yes," he said politely.

"Nice to meet you. I'm Virginia, Izzy's mother." Her eyes immediately fell on the cut over his eye. "Ooh. What happened there?"

He smiled disarmingly. "Wasn't looking where I was going."

"Goodness," she said, in an airy sort of way. She led him down a hallway and into the main living area, which was magnificently huge; it was all open, and there was a gigantic stairway (with golden bannisters) right in the middle of it, leading up to a second level. "Izzy's still getting ready. Please, make yourself comfortable."

He sat down on a sofa, feeling kind of awkward. A moment later, Izzy's father, Edmund Rushforth, appeared as well; he was a serious, unsmiling character who Kaden thought looked a little like Gregory Peck, if Gregory Peck was having a particularly bad day. He was wearing a black suit and thick, black-rimmed glasses. "Hello," the man said, nodding at him rather perfunctorily.

Kaden immediately got up and shook his hand. "Kaden Ely," he said. "Pleasure to meet you."

"You're the Daniels boy, aren't you?" Izzy's father asked, peering at him over the rims of his glasses. "The one he adopted?"

"Quentin Daniels is my foster father, yes."

"Mr. Daniels has a bit of a wild streak."

"Umm...yes." The random remark had thrown him off a bit. "Of course you can't believe everything you read in the tabloids—"

He was cut off by a couple of barking dogs, who suddenly came racing down the stairs, heading right for him. One was a yellow lab; the other was some kind of beagle. The beagle jumped up on the sofa and tried to lick his face.

"Oh, get off him, you two!" Izzy's mother ordered, herding the dogs into another room. "For heaven's sake. I'm sorry about that. Izzy's never really bothered to train these two."

"They're Izzy's dogs?"

"Two of the three," her father said, rolling his eyes. "This place is a zoo."

"She has a lot of pets," Virginia agreed, sighing. "The dogs, plus three cats, a cockatiel, a turtle, and a terrarium full of tree frogs."

"Oh," Kaden said, amused. "I didn't know. She never mentioned them to me."

Virginia gave him a critical look. "How did you two meet?"

"We, umm...we worked on a history project together." And then, to score some points, he added, "It was Izzy who did most of the work, though."

"Well, that's good to hear."

Kaden was starting to get a little uncomfortable. Izzy's parents were friendly enough, he supposed, but he obviously hadn't impressed her father, and although she seemed pleasant, there was something severe about her mother. It was in the eyes, he thought. Mother and daughter both had blue eyes, which looked very much alike, but if Izzy's eyes were cool, her mother's were ice-cold. He wondered how the two of them got along.

"So what kind of career are you looking at, son?" Edmund Rushforth suddenly asked. "I assume Daniels is getting something lined up for you."

"You could say that," Kaden replied cautiously.

"Business, is it? Or were you considering law school?" His eyes were narrowing into slits.

Kaden squirmed a bit, but was saved by Izzy's mother: "Ah," she said, looking to the grand stairway. "Here's Izzy, at last."

A relieved Kaden turned his gaze to the top of the stairs...and his mouth fell open.

Izzy, of course, was lovely even in her school uniform, but she was *beyond* lovely tonight, and all the way into stunning. She was wearing a lacy, navy-blue gown, with golden bracelets on her wrists and the strap of a small, gold-sequined purse slung over one bare shoulder. Her light-blonde hair, which she usually wore straight, had been curled into ringlets, and she was wearing earrings, which he'd never seen her wear before. Heels, too.

"Hi," she said, a little shyly, as she descended the stairs.

"Hi," Kaden returned. "You look great."

"Thanks. You clean up pretty good yourself."

"I should get a picture," Izzy's mother said, pulling out her phone.

"Oh, come on, Mom," Izzy complained, obviously embarrassed. "It's not like we're going to the *prom*. This is just a dance."

"It's a special occasion," she insisted. "When's the last time you went to a dance? Come on, now. Smile, you two."

Kaden glanced at Izzy. "When *was* the last time you went to a dance?"

"Just shut up and let her take the stupid picture," she grumbled.

* * *

"Nice car," Izzy said, as they climbed into the Ferrari.

"It's Quentin's. I prefer bikes myself. Let's see...the best way to the Lexington 405..."

"I'd probably take 10th Street," she said. "Into Cruciform Plaza, and then south."

"Right, right." He checked his mirrors and slipped into traffic.

"Sorry about my parents," Izzy said, after a moment of awkward silence. "I told you they'd make a big deal out of it."

"They weren't *that* bad. Your father was a little scary, maybe, but I'm guessing all fathers are like that around their daughters' dates. I was a little more surprised by the dogs. You didn't tell me you had any pets."

"Oh. Well, I do. Dogs, cats, birds, frogs..."

"You must really like animals, huh?"

"Yeah." She gave him a nervous, sideways sort of smile. "Actually...I'd like to be a veterinarian."

"Really?" He thought about that. "I can see that. It's funny, but, yeah, I can see you as a vet. So are you planning on going to school for it?"

"I said I'd *like* to be a vet," she said, the smile fading. "I didn't say I was *going* to be."

"Why not? What's stopping you?"

"My parents," she said simply.

"They don't want you to be a vet?"

She shook her head. "They want me to take a position at Rushforth International after I graduate from college. They'd laugh, if I told them I wanted to be a vet."

"They want you to run the company?"

She snorted. "I'm sure they'd like that. No, I don't think they expect me to take over for my father. But they want me working for the company in *some* capacity; they've been telling me that since I was a toddler. I *have* to work for RI. It's my...destiny."

"I thought your destiny was to be a hero."

She said nothing in reply to that, but turned her gaze towards the window.

"I don't think your parents should be making *all* of your decisions," Kaden volunteered.

"They run my life," she said, her breath fogging up the window.

"*You* run your life," he said firmly. "You don't have to do anything you don't want to do, Izzy."

"Don't be stupid. Sometimes we're stuck, doing things we don't want to do. Sometimes we have no choice."

"No. No, that's wrong. You *always* have a choice." He nodded at a traffic light, up ahead. "I don't *have* to stop at this red light, for example. I could go right through it if I wanted to."

"You'd get us in an accident."

"Maybe," Kaden agreed. "There'd be consequences, certainly— there's *always* consequences, when we refuse to do things we'd rather not do. But the decision, for better or worse, is always *yours* to make; no one can take that away from you. In life, you can run all the red lights you want."

She snorted at that, too. "That's easy for you to say, when *you're* the one behind the wheel."

They made it to the Lexington 405 a few minutes later, and took the elevator up to the party. The dance was being held in a large, glittering ballroom, on the upper floors of the Lexington building, and it was already in full swing by the time they arrived. Most of their classmates, all dressed to the nines, were sipping on punch and chatting amiably with one another, but a few were on the floor, dancing to the live music—a goth-rock band, which sounded a little like Evanescence, was on a stage, performing a slow song. Multicolored lights had been arranged all around the enormous room, and the view out the floor-to-ceiling windows was spectacular. The whole of the city was spread out before them.

They were met at the elevator by Mr. and Mrs. Kronkenburger —the chaperones—and by Luke Mahajan, the class president, who thanked them for coming, told them where to find the punch, and promptly ran off to make a phone call (he seemed like a pretty busy guy). Kaden and Izzy entered the room, a little apprehensive.

"So...what do we do?" Izzy whispered.

"We have fun," he said uncertainly. "I guess. Do you want some punch?"

"I suppose."

They made their way over to the refreshments, got some punch...and stood there, uncomfortably, for several minutes, wondering what to do with themselves. They were finally saved by Race, who spotted them from the dance floor and immediately came over to greet them. Kaden had never been happier to see anyone in his life.

"Hi, Kaden," he said cheerily. "You having fun?"

"Time of my life. Izzy, this is Race; you've probably seen him around. He's a friend of mine."

"Nice to meet you," she said.

"Likewise." He gave Kaden a nudge. "I thought you told me school dances weren't your thing."

He shrugged. "What can I say? Izzy begged me."

She reddened. "I did not *beg* you," she said, through gritted teeth. "You'd better not spread that around."

"You're here together, then? Is this a date?"

Kaden glanced at Izzy. "I suppose you could call it a—"

"Hey! Ely!"

All three of them turned towards the speaker—who, to Kaden's dismay, turned out to be Russell Lachmiller. The giant, dressed up in a huge tuxedo (he looked ridiculous in it; the tux was at least two sizes too small) was stomping over to them, clearing a path through the crowd.

Uh-oh.

Kaden wasn't afraid of Russell—he felt certain he could beat him up again, if he had to—but he had no desire to make a scene. He glanced at Izzy, looking for a little guidance, but she merely shrugged.

Russell stopped in front of him. "Ely," he grunted, by way of greeting. He still had a bandage on his nose.

"Russell," Kaden returned, nodding.

The big guy looked down at him for a moment...and then extended a hand for him to shake. "I, umm, I just wanted to say sorry, for coming at you like that the other day."

Kaden, surprised at this turn of events, studied him carefully. Russell looked sincere, so he shook the senior's giant mitt, and said, "No problem. Apology accepted."

"Good, good. We're okay, then? Good." He shook his big, shaved head in a dejected sort of way. "I don't usually go around picking fights, I want you to know. Angel...she put me up to it."

"I figured."

"We're not together anymore," he added.

"Oh." Scanning the room, Kaden spotted a furious-looking Angel standing over by the band, staring daggers at the whole group. Yikes. "Russell, this is Izzy, and this is Race."

"Hi, hi."

"How's your nose?" Race inquired. "Still hurt?"

"Nah. Hurt like hell for a while there, though. That was a mad kick, man; I never saw it coming. You think you could teach me some of those moves?"

"Sure," Kaden said, "if you're willing to learn."

Russell, as it turned out, may have been a little dim, but he was actually a pretty friendly guy. The four of them had a nice, long chat at the refreshment table, which helped Kaden and Izzy both start to feel a bit more at ease. Race, for his part, wasted no time in turning the conversation towards his favorite subject: superheroes.

"Hypnotika was seen in Stone's Row again," he said. "Last night. That's what they're saying online, anyway. Oh! And did you hear about Nightdragon? He almost captured Ma Crime the day before yesterday. Sparkler Girl was there, too; apparently there was a huge fight down in Friars. I've been trying to find some footage on YouTube. Did you hear about it?"

"'Fraid not," Kaden said. And this was true; he'd been much too preoccupied lately to worry about what Signal City's *other* heroes had been getting up to.

"I think I heard about that," Russell said, scratching his head. "Wasn't Missy Mischief there, too?"

Kaden's ears pricked up. Missy Mischief? Yvette?

"Yeah, yeah! I guess she must be working for Ma Crime. Nightdragon was fighting her. Have you ever seen him fight?"

Kaden had, in fact, seen Nightdragon fight, and in person—the superhero frequently ran afoul of the Dark, and Skirmish and

Quarterstaff had crossed paths with him several times. His insistence on fighting bare-handed had always struck Kaden as a little silly, but the man's skill was undeniable.

This mention of Missy Mischief was much more interesting to him, though. Yvette Lemieux was...well, not a friend, exactly, but he used to see her around the Matsumoto Academy all the time—she'd finished her training five or six years ahead of him, but had continued to drop by the Academy for years afterward (usually looking for work, or for a place to crash). Though she was several years older than them, Kaden and Rio had both had crushes on her—crushes which she'd gone out of her way to encourage. Yvette was a shameless flirt.

She was also a highly skilled martial artist, who'd gone mercenary after leaving the Academy. She'd been captured a few years ago, by the superheroine Vermillion, but had managed to escape police custody; the last Kaden had heard, she'd been hiding out somewhere in the French Riviera. Now, apparently, she was back in Signal City. Interesting.

"I've seen Nightdragon on TV a few times," Russell was saying. "Good fighter. I bet Ely here could give him a run for his money, though!" He chuckled.

"Yeah," Kaden said, smiling uneasily. "Right."

The band started a new song about then, and Russell left them to hang out with some of his wrestling buddies. Race, too, ran off, headed for the bathroom, leaving Kaden and Izzy alone once again.

"I guess he's not so bad," Kaden said, about Russell, "once you get to know him."

"I guess."

Another awkward silence followed; they sipped on their punch. Finally, unable to bear it any longer, Kaden turned to Izzy. "Everyone else is dancing," he pointed out.

"Yeah."

"Do *you* want to dance?"

"With you?"

He stared. "No, with Mr. Kronkenburger. Of *course* with me!"

"Okay, okay. Let's dance, then. I mean, if you insist."

He took her by the hand and led her out onto the floor. The band was playing a slow number, so they danced a slow dance, amidst the other couples, while starry lights sparkled overhead. The female singer—a pale, eyeshadowy woman with a Skrillex haircut—was singing about death and tragedy. Kaden caught a whiff of Izzy's perfume; it smelled nice.

Something was bothering him, though. "This is kind of embarrassing," he said quietly, after a moment.

"What is?"

"You're taller than me in heels."

She looked down at her shoes. "Oh. Is that a problem?"

"You don't mind?"

She affected to think about it. "No. No, I don't mind."

They danced some more. At length, the band wrapped up the slow number and took a break; Kaden and Izzy stepped back from one another. "That was...nice," Izzy said.

"Yeah," Kaden agreed, the smell of her perfume still in his nostrils. "Nice."

"This isn't a date, you know," she added.

He'd just opened his mouth to respond to this when Race, standing near the floor-to-ceiling windows, suddenly shouted out: "Hey!" he exclaimed, eyes wide. "Look at *that!*"

Kaden glanced out the window...and started. A strange, pulsating *blob* of red light, spitting out bolts of red-orange electricity, had materialized on the horizon, about two or three miles from where they stood. The light, whatever it was, was gigantic, and it appeared to be hovering over a distant skyscraper. Kaden, along with everyone else in the room, stared at the weird, mysterious light in wide-eyed wonder, but after a moment it became too bright to look at, and he was forced to look away. The orb was illuminating the entire skyline, limning the buildings with its light.

"What the hell...?"

And then the lights went out in the ballroom. The Jeffries students, alarmed, began shouting out in fear and surprise, and looking to one another for answers. Several immediately took their phones out, to film the strange light and to check the Internet for an explanation as to what was going on.

Mr. Kronkenburger appeared, waving his arms to get everyone's attention. "All right now, calm down, calm down." He gave the red light an annoyed, sideways glance. "Everybody just relax and hang tight here for a few minutes, while we figure out what's going on."

Meanwhile, the bizarre light continued to pulsate, but it was throwing out a whole range of colors now; pinks, purples, and oranges flashed across the horizon. It looked like some kind of crazy, electrical sunset, and it was actually rather pretty.

Izzy turned to Kaden. "Any idea what's going on?"

"No."

"What do you think that light is?"

He shrugged. "Magic, maybe? I don't know."

After a few minutes, Race was able to give them an update. "Power's out over half the city," he said, tapping away at his phone. "*Champions Weekly* just got a statement from the Paranormals— apparently that light is some kind of magical beacon, put up by a group of Abyssos-worshippers. You know Abyssos, right?"

Kaden frowned. "Some kind of demon, isn't he?"

"Yeah. His acolytes are always scheming to bring him to Earth. Looks like this is their latest plot. Anyway, the Paranormals are on their way, and the Signal Corps shouldn't be far behind. Probably Shieldmaiden and the Ancient Greek will get mixed up in there, too."

"Well, that's a relief."

"What do you think?" Izzy asked him, in a low voice. "Should we go? The Paranormals might need some help."

Kaden gave the magical light show a doubtful look. "I think we're stuck here. It'd take forever to get over to that light, with the city blacked out. If the traffic lights are down–"

"I can fly," she reminded him. "Sort of."

"*I* can't. Could you carry me?"

She hesitated. "I'm not sure."

"We'd probably just get in the way, anyway. The Paranormals know what they're doing, and if the Signal Corps is on its way as well..." He shrugged. "That's a lot of firepower. They can *probably* handle this."

It turned into a moot point, anyway; the elevators weren't working, and Mr. Kronkenburger wasn't about to let anyone take the stairs. "We're all going to remain here," he said firmly, "until this thing blows over. Might as well make yourselves comfortable. There's plenty of food left, and plenty of punch, and...hey! Martinez! Stop fooling around with that thing!"

It became a very strange evening. With nothing to do but check their phones and wait for the power to come back on, the Jeffries students—who soon found themselves transfixed by the beauty of the pulsating blob of light—settled themselves down along the floor-to-ceiling windows and spent the next several hours quietly watching the pyrotechnics flash across the horizon. There wasn't much *fear*—crises of this sort were fairly common in Signal City, after all, and most everyone was more or less accustomed to them—but there *was* a great deal of nervous excitement; the students spoke to each other in whispers, *oohing* and *ahhing* occasionally at the changes in the lights. It was something like a watching a thunderstorm, or a fireworks display.

Kaden and Izzy sat down to watch the lights as well, but apart from the others, so that they might not be overheard.

"What are they like?" Izzy asked. "The Paranormals, I mean. You've met them, haven't you?"

"Yeah, a few times. They're nice enough. Pretty odd bunch, though; their leader is a seven-foot-tall demon-guy, with horns and a pointy tail. Pitchfork, they call him."

"And the others?"

"Enchantryn's a sorceress, one of the best in the world. Kid Phantom can turn invisible. Spirit-Man can switch bodies with just about anybody, and the Alakazammer...well, he used to be a stage magician, and he's more of a showman than anything, but he's got plenty of tricks up his sleeves—he defeated the Pyromech, once, by turning his flamethrowers into flowers. I still don't know how he pulled *that* one off. Anyway, I'm sure they'll do fine against these cultists, or whatever they are." He glanced at her. "Did you want to meet them? They work out of a dreary old library in Stone's Row—Alcott, I think it's called. I could take you over there sometime, introduce you. I have a feeling they'd be very interested in that cloak of yours. Heck, they might even ask you to join the team."

"Maybe," she said softly. "Maybe someday."

They were quiet for a moment, contemplating the lights. "You know what this reminds me of?" Kaden asked, after an especially flashy flare-up. "The Externian Invasion."

"I was in Europe when that happened."

"Oh. Well, it was pretty strange stuff. The whole city went crazy. There were all these lights in the sky, and monsters and giant castles started popping up out of thin air all over the place. *Very* weird night."

"How'd you spend it?"

He sighed. "Stuck in a hospital. It was only two days after my fight with Rio. But I had a great view of it all, out my window...just like tonight."

"It's pretty," she commented, as the lights splashed her face.

"Yeah," Kaden said. "Pretty." But he wasn't looking at the lights.

Another half-hour passed. It was well after midnight now, and Izzy, obviously drowsy, began nodding off. She fought it as long as she could (while Kaden watched her, quietly amused), but eventually it caught up with her, and she fell forward, her head lolling into her chest. Kaden, wrapping an arm around her, put her upright again, and without waking up she melted into his side, her blonde head coming to rest on his shoulder.

He looked down at her, studying her delicate features, and then, on impulse, lowered his head and whispered into her ear, "Izzy. Wake up."

She woke up, her eyes opening in a slow, languid sort of way. He expected her to pull away from him, upon realizing how close they were, but she didn't; instead, she gave him a puzzled look, and the two of them proceeded to stare at each other, silently, for a long moment. A long, *long* moment.

Their faces were only inches apart.

Kaden was seized by another impulse. He drew her closer, leaned down, and...

And *then* she pulled away, disentangling herself from his arms and setting herself upright. "I'm sorry," she said, fixing her hair. "That was...that was..." She was taking great care not to look him in the eye.

"That was what?" Kaden wondered.

But he never got an answer, because at that moment, the fireworks display ended in a magnificent starburst of golden light. The Jeffries students—the ones who weren't too busy making out, at any rate—applauded.

"They did it!" Race exclaimed, checking his phone. "The Paranormals did it!"

The power came back on a few minutes later, and Mr. Kronkenburger, after consulting with the building's security, gave his students the all-clear to leave. A few die-hards hung around, but most quickly headed for the elevators and began making their way home.

Kaden and Izzy returned to the Ferrari. The ride back to Izzy's building was uncomfortably awkward; Izzy seemed lost in her own world, and Kaden, confused and embarrassed, didn't know what to say.

They arrived back at the Madison Building at about two in the morning. "Here we are," Kaden said, having parked the car.

She didn't get out. "Yeah."

"Some dance, huh? Memorable, anyway."

"Yeah."

Kaden frowned. "Look, Izzy, I don't know if I did something wrong, or if *we* did something wrong, or what, but I'm pretty sure that—"

"I lied to you."

He stopped. "What?"

"I lied. I didn't get the Ribbon from an old Chinese lady in Shanghai. I made all that up."

He hadn't seen *this* coming. "You made it up?"

She nodded quietly, eyes downcast.

"So...where *did* you get it?"

"I bought it. I bought it in California, from a supervillain called the Iron Skull. He has hundreds of magical artifacts in his collection, really powerful ones, and for the right price..." She shrugged her bare shoulders. "He's willing to sell them."

"You bought the Ribbon from a supervillain? How...how much did it cost?"

"You don't want to know."

Kaden absorbed this. "You're confusing me, Izzy. You're telling me you cut a deal with a supervillain, to get your hands on a magic cloak? Why?"

"Because I wanted to make myself a superhero." She finally deigned to look at him; her eyes were just beginning to fill with tears. "Remember what you told me yesterday, about how you were afraid you didn't become a superhero because you wanted to do good, but just because you liked to fight?" She laughed bitterly. "I'm no better. I didn't become a hero because some little old lady told me it was my destiny, or because I had some strong desire to help people. I bought the Ribbon, and became a superhero, because I wanted a second life —a life of my *own*. I've told you how controlling my parents are, how they have everything planned out for me. Isidora Rushforth *has* to listen to her parents, *has* to do what they say...but the White Ribbon *doesn't*. The Ribbon is free. *She* makes her own decisions. *She* runs the red lights."

Kaden was surprised, maybe even a little stunned, by this confession...but he thought he understood. "You wanted another identity," he said slowly. "A secret identity."

She nodded. "I could have a second life, as a superhero. That's what I thought. I could go out at night, fight crime, meet other heroes...I could have my *own* life, apart from the one my parents had planned for me." She hung her head. "Unfortunately the White Ribbon has just as hard a time making friends as Izzy Rushforth does. The only other hero I've met is you, and *you* discovered my other identity right away."

"Ah," he said, drumming his fingers against the steering wheel. "I'm getting it now. *That's* why you didn't want to work together at first. You wanted one life for Izzy, and another for the White Ribbon. You wanted to keep them separate, but you *couldn't* keep them separate around me, because *I* knew your secret."

"Perceptive," she muttered. "The fact that you knew who I was...I didn't like that. I wanted to keep my distance from you. But I needed your help finding Olivia, and then we started working together on that history project, and then...and then *tonight*."

"Yeah. Tonight." He looked at her evenly. "And you're still trying to keep your distance from me, aren't you?"

"I'm afraid," she said, very softly. "I *bought* my way into this life. I became a superhero for the wrong reasons, Kaden; I've felt like a phony from the beginning. Until I know for certain that I'm *worthy* of all this, that I'm not just doing it for *me*, I'm afraid...I'm afraid of getting too caught up in it." She looked at him. "Do you understand?"

"Not really," he said, but actually, he sort of did. Izzy was having doubts about this new life she'd created for herself...and because *he* was a part of that life, she was wary of getting close to him.

He could relate to the rest of it, too. Neither of them had become crime fighters for purely altruistic reasons; they'd both had ulterior motives. Both were afraid that they weren't real heroes.

They were more alike than he'd realized.

"I'm sorry," Izzy said. "I guess...I guess I must sound pretty screwed up." She wiped away a tear. "Maybe because I *am*."

Kaden sighed. "Welcome to the club."

CHAPTER TWELVE

Kaden's own feelings were clear—he liked Izzy, and he was liking her more all the time. He wasn't so sure about *her* feelings, though, and as she seemed to want some space (or some time, at least, to figure out how she felt), he only spoke with her a few times over the following week. Nevertheless, rumors about them began circulating almost immediately after the dance—or so Race informed him.

"Everyone thinks you're together now," he told Kaden at lunch. "What's the story? You two were all lovey-dovey at the dance–"

"We weren't lovey-dovey."

"You *looked* lovey-dovey."

Kaden's eyes narrowed. "If you use that word one more time, Race, I swear–"

"Okay, okay. Sorry. So what's going on? Are you dating or what?"

He frowned. "No. I don't think so."

"You don't *think* so?"

"It's complicated."

Race shrugged, and returned to his magazine—another issue of *Sixgun's Metahuman Review.* "Whatever." And then he added, offhandedly, "She's pretty, and she's not stuck-up, either, like everyone says she is. You could do a lot worse than Izzy Rushforth."

* * *

Though distracted by this drama with Izzy, and still recovering from the beating he'd received in Al Muranaka's apartment, Kaden nevertheless continued his pursuit of Rio and the Dark over the next few days. Stuck for leads, however, he failed to make any real progress, and after spinning his wheels a while he decided to contact Sly a second time. Kaden was almost certain his old teacher knew where the Dark was hiding the Matsumoto Academy, and though it might take some convincing, he was pretty sure he could get it out of him.

Sly failed to answer his phone, however, and so, on a cold Wednesday night, Kaden threw on a coat, got on his motorcycle, and headed over to his apartment to talk to him in person.

Upon arriving at his brownstone, in Stone's Row, Kaden climbed the carpeted stairs and knocked on the man's door. There was no answer, so he knocked again. Still no answer.

He'd probably just stepped out, to pick up groceries or take in a movie or something...but the fact that he wasn't home, coupled with the fact that he hadn't been answering his phone all day, aroused Kaden's suspicion. Frowning, he exited the building, acrobatted his way up a series of ledges, and peered into one of Sly's windows.

Unfortunately, the shades were drawn. Still suspicious, and, if he was being honest, a little worried about his friend, he knifed the lock open, pulled the window up, and slipped inside.

He was half expecting to stumble upon another murder scene, but, to his relief, there was nothing amiss in Sly's apartment—everything was as it had been the last time Kaden had been there. Apparently his teacher *had* simply stepped out.

Feeling a little foolish, Kaden returned to the window. He stopped briefly at Sly's desk, however, chuckling at the sight of a large binder with the words "Confidence Realty" emblazoned on the cover. He was still having a hard time envisioning Sly as a real estate agent.

Leaving the building, Kaden climbed back on his motorcycle and drove around a bit, trying to organize his thoughts. He needed to get closer to the Dark and their operation, if he was to have any hope of finding out what they were up to. And to do that, he needed to find and begin surveilling the Matsumoto Academy. What was required here was some good old fashioned detective work.

How to find their headquarters, though? He supposed he could rough up some of their low-level kneecappers, but even they might not be privy to the Academy's current location, which was usually a closely-guarded secret. He supposed, as well, that he could try tracking down one of the Academy's instructors...but the instructors were *dangerous*, and if they discovered they were being shadowed...well, he didn't want the Dark alert to the fact that he was investigating them.

There had to be *somebody* out there with the intel he needed, though. Someone with a connection to the Dark, willing to talk to him, but who wouldn't immediately rat him out.

A connection to the Dark...

And then, all at once, it hit him: Yvette.

Grinning, he popped a wheelie, veered south, and headed for Steelworks.

* * *

It was a lovely penthouse. Yvette, who had a peculiar fascination with the antebellum South, had filled it up with lush curtains, carved oak furniture, and gilded-age mirrors and makeup tables, all of which looked like they'd been pilfered from the set of *Gone with the Wind*. But there were modern touches as well—a laptop, charging on one of the vanities; an MP3 player lying carelessly on the red-velvet couch; and, most incongruously, a set of 9mm handguns, which for some reason were sitting on her kitchen counter. There were swords, knives, claws, and other, more exotic weapons (Yvette was partial to umbrella swords) scattered about the living room as well.

Kaden, after inspecting the apartment, hid himself behind one of her enormous curtains and patiently waited for her to return home. It was a long wait; he broke into her place around ten-thirty, and she didn't appear until almost midnight.

When out and about as Missy Mischief, Yvette's preferred costume was a hoop skirt, with knee-high boots and a flowered hat, and she usually carried a lacy parasol as well (which doubled as a weapon). She wasn't wearing any of that tonight, though; she entered her apartment wearing ordinary street clothes, and with her brown hair in a bun. Evidently she was trying to keep a lower profile.

Locking the door behind her, Yvette—obviously rather tired—stretched her arms out lazily, threw her keys on the coffee table, and let out a big yawn.

She had her back to him. Kaden pulled the curtain aside. "Long time no see."

She spun around. In one smooth motion, she removed a hairstick from her bun and threw it at him, with near-perfect precision. Kaden had been expecting something like this, though, and had no trouble dodging the projectile, which stuck itself in the curtain. Surging forward, he managed to grab her by the wrist and pull her into him, allowing her a close-up of his face. "Now, now," he said, "is that any way to greet an old friend?"

She continued to struggle, but stopped when she recognized him. "Little K? Is that you?"

"I wish you wouldn't call me that," he grumbled, releasing her arm.

Her eyes lit up. "It *is* you!" And then she threw her arms around his neck and gave him a huge hug, pressing her impressively voluptuous body up against him. "Oh, it's been *ages!*"

He'd expected the projectile; he *hadn't* expected this. "It's good to see you too, Yvette," he managed.

"Look at you! All grown up! What are you doing here? That was a hell of a fright you gave me, babe; you're lucky I didn't perforate you."

"Please. I saw that one coming a mile away."

"Oh, get out of here," she said, pushing him away playfully. "How'd you find me?"

"Heard you were working for Ma Crime," he said. "I found one of her goons, convinced him to give me your address."

She frowned. "How much *convincing* did it take?"

"Not much."

She shook her head, disgusted. "It's hard to find good goons these days. I don't think that fat old woman is paying them enough." She brightened. "So what are you *doing* here, sugar? Gosh, I haven't seen you since...how long has it been?"

"It's three years, now, since I left the Academy."

"Yeah, yeah! I heard about that. You had some kind of falling-out with Rio, right?" She winked at him. "I suppose you two playboys were fighting over *me.*"

He gave her an indulgent smile. "Of course."

"So what happened to you, after that?"

He shrugged. "Nothing too dramatic. Fell into a pretty normal life, actually. Believe it or not I even go to school now, like a totally normal kid."

She winced. "You have my sympathies."

"And what've *you* been up to?"

It was her turn to shrug. "Same old. Ma Crime's got me under contract for another couple of months. I can't wait to get out of this one; I *hate* that stupid woman. She's got a *lousy* organization. Her idiot son managed to screw up a perfectly ordinary job a few days ago—almost got me killed."

"You're talking about the fight with Nightdragon?"

"You heard about that? Yeah, that was the one. Whole thing just *erupted*." She dismissed the subject with a wave. "You still haven't told me what you're doing here."

"Actually," he said, "I have a favor to ask."

"Oh?"

He nodded. "I've been thinking...I may have made a mistake, in leaving the Academy. I'm thinking about going back and finishing my training...if they'll have me."

"Starting to get tired of the normal life, huh?"

"You could say that."

"They seemed pretty sore about your leaving," she said doubtfully. "I have a feeling you'll have to do some serious sucking up to get back in."

"Yeah, I kinda figured."

"So what do you need from me?"

"I was hoping you could tell me where they're keeping the Academy these days."

She smiled impishly. "That's supposed to be a secret."

"Do you know where it is?"

"Oh, yes. It's been a few months since I dropped by, but I'd have heard if they'd moved it."

"Great. Can you give me the address?"

"Of course I *could*, but..." Her voice became coy. "They'd be *very* cross with me, you know, if they found out I gave it to you. They might stop inviting me to their Christmas parties."

"Yvette..."

"All right. I'll tell you where they are...but only on one condition."

He raised an eyebrow. "What condition?"

There appeared a mischievous glint in her eye. "Little K. All grown up." She touched her tongue to her upper lip (*very* suggestively), took a step towards him, and *slowly* wrapped her arms around his neck again. "I've had a long day, kiddo," she whispered into his ear. "I need to unwind."

Kaden swallowed. "Yvette, I...I..."

"What's the matter?" she purred. "Don't you like me?"

"I've...I've got a girlfriend." This wasn't strictly true, but it came to him quickly, as a handy excuse. Yvette, however, was unimpressed. "So?" She looked him in the eye, all smoky and seductive, raised her chin, moved her lips close to his...

...And then burst out laughing.

Kaden was confused. "What? What was...?"

"Oh, that was *too* funny," she said, pulling away from him. "The look on your face—priceless! You haven't changed at all, Kaden. You're as uptight as ever."

She'd been toying with him. Of course. Kaden groaned.

He supposed he should've expected it; after all, they didn't call her Missy Mischief for nothing.

* * *

Yvette did, eventually, provide him with the Academy's new address: the Dark was training their new recruits, she told him, in an old boxing gym on 47th and Crawford, and housing them in a basement apartment nearby. Kaden thanked her for the information and immediately began making plans to surveil the place. After scouting the area, and finding a small, nondescript parking lot across the street, he loaded up one of Quentin's SUV's with some covert listening equipment—a parabolic microphone and a nonlinear acoustic enhancer—and got to work. He had some experience with this sort of thing; his instructors at the Academy had given him a few spying lessons back in the day, and Quentin, more recently, had provided him with a bit of training as well.

The Dark were masters of clandestine operations, though, and any attempt to spy on them, without their catching on, was going to be difficult. He took a cautious approach over the next two evenings, parking in different spots, using different vehicles, and keeping a very close eye on their lookout, whom he spotted almost immediately. They had him dressed like a panhandler, but his constant, furtive glances, up and down the street, gave the game away.

Many of the voices he heard over the headphones were familiar to him. He recognized Yeng's voice, and Edge's; the two of them were always shouting angrily at their students. He heard Fan, grumbling to himself in his workshop. He heard the Gao twins, drinking late into the night, and he heard Patch terrify a new student with the story of his missing eye. To Kaden, it felt like...well, much as he hated to admit it, listening to all those familiar voices made him feel almost homesick.

Unfortunately, for the instructors, the Academy was more of a hangout than a headquarters, and they tended to avoid talking business there. Two days passed, and he heard nothing about the stolen weapons, nor any hint that the Dark might be behind the Stone's Row disappearances. Most of the instructors' conversations with each other were entirely mundane, and Kaden soon began to despair of ever hearing anything useful.

On the third day of his surveillance, late in the afternoon, he received a call from Izzy. "Hello?"

"Hi, Kaden. Are you busy? I've got some news." She sounded pretty excited.

"I'm not busy. What've you got?"

"A break in the kidnapping case. At least, I *hope* it's a break. Remember that girl Mariana—the one who went missing in Cincinnatus Park?"

"I remember."

"Well, a witness just came forward who saw what happened to her. The SCPD released a statement a few hours ago; it's on their website."

He started. "A witness?"

"Yeah, a seven-year-old kid named Dylan. He was a friend of Mariana's; they were playing together in the park that night. Apparently he didn't come forward earlier because he didn't want to get in trouble—he wasn't supposed to have been out that late."

"Okay, so what did he see? What happened to Mariana?"

"She got into a van," Izzy said. "A woman talked her into getting in, and drove off with her."

"A woman?"

"Yeah. Dylan described her as...let's see..." She paused, evidently looking for the relevant paragraph on her computer screen. "He said she was a pretty woman, with dark hair and a funny accent. She scared him—that's another reason he didn't come forward right away. He hid behind the playground equipment while the woman talked to Mariana."

"A dark-haired woman with a funny accent, huh? What *kind* of funny accent?"

"He didn't specify."

"Too bad."

"What do you think? Do you think she could've been working for the Dark? Do you have any idea who this woman could be?"

"Not really," Kaden said. "No one *I* know fits that description."

She sighed. "Shoot."

"Did the kid have anything else to say? What color was the van?"

"White. And that's actually consistent with another one of the kidnappings—Luis Lopez was seen talking to someone in a white van right before *he* was abducted, too. This would seem to confirm Detective Arroyo's theory, about all these kidnappings being connected."

"Luis Lopez?"

"One of the missing kids," she explained. "I've been looking into the cases—or trying to, anyway. Luis disappeared from a convenience store parking lot back in May, after buying a bottle of Coca-Cola. The clerk who sold it to him was the one who reported seeing the white van."

The name "Lopez" rang a bell. Where had he heard that name before?

And then it hit him: the name had appeared in Arroyo's handwritten note, the one Kaden had rescued from his wastepaper basket: "Check witness account, Lopez case, possible link to Armitage robbery." He'd very nearly forgotten about that note.

Arroyo had thought he had found a link between the robbery at the Armitage auction house and the kidnapping of Luis Lopez. *That* was why he'd been investigating both sets of cases, Kaden suddenly realized—he'd believed that the thefts and the kidnappings were related. Somehow or other, Arroyo had come to the conclusion that the thieves, stealing the enchanted weapons, and the kidnappers, stealing the unwary children, were one and the same.

He was just about to relate all this to Izzy when, out of the corner of his eye, he suddenly spotted a black SUV pull up and park in front of the gym.

Two men stepped out of the vehicle: Rio, and a short Japanese man in his mid-sixties, with wavy white hair, wearing big square spectacles and a loud Hawaiian shirt.

Sho Matsumoto. The Darkest.

No one, looking at this unassuming man, would believe that he was a criminal mastermind, let alone one of the deadliest martial artists in the world. He looked completely harmless, which, Kaden supposed, was probably the point.

Rio opened the door for Matsumoto, and both entered the building. Kaden, after saying goodbye to Izzy, quickly fired up the microphones, and almost immediately, heard Rio's voice over his headphones. "Can I get you anything, sir?" he asked his boss.

"Not right now," Matsumoto replied. His voice, which belied his looks, was deep and menacing. "Bring them out. I'd like to have a look at them."

The Dark's newest recruits were duly brought out, to be inspected by the Darkest. He spoke to the students briefly and watched a few of them spar. Then, apparently satisfied, he dismissed the instructors and sat down to have a one-on-one talk with Rio. Kaden had trouble hearing the conversation—his microphone was giving him problems—but the bits and pieces he did manage to pick up were intriguing.

"...as easy as finding the Satsujinken," Matsumoto was saying.

"I'm sorry," Rio replied, apologetic.

"I don't want you to be sorry," Matsumoto growled. "I want you to find my sword."

"I understand. I just need a little more time."

"You *are* making progress?"

"Of course. I'm going out tonight, in fact, to follow up on–" His voice was then drowned out by static, only to return a moment later: "–but I don't think he actually had anything to do with it. I'll find out tonight, if I'm being played."

"I want this thief *found*, Killian. It's been two months now, since the break-in. That a thief could enter *my* home, and steal *my* sword...and I gave you this task, because...from overseas..." More static, and it took Kaden several seconds to adjust the microphone. By the time he got it going again, Rio was speaking: "–won't let you down, sir."

Matsumoto snorted. "Best not."

Alas, the rest of the conversation was a garbled mess. Frustrated, Kaden turned off the listening equipment and, as it was getting rather late, called it a day. Climbing back into the front seat, he pulled out of the parking lot and began making his way back to Daniels Tower.

As he drove, he reflected on what he'd just heard. The upshot of it seemed to be that the Satsujinken had been stolen from Matsumoto's collection, and that Rio had been ordered to recover it.

Who in the world would be stupid enough to steal from the Darkest? And the Satsujinken...

Kaden frowned. Rio, he now recalled, had all but accused *him* of stealing the Satsujinken, that night on the baseball field.

What could possibly have led him to *that* conclusion? He hadn't thought much about Rio's accusation at the time, but it struck him as strange now.

And that wasn't the only thing bothering him. The Satsujinken was no ordinary sword; it was an *enchanted* blade, rumored to have been forged out of a chunk of meteorite by the demented Japanese swordsmith Iga Komatsu over six hundred years ago. It was a magic sword, with magic in the steel.

And it had been stolen.

Huh.

Kaden had been convinced, from the very beginning, that the Dark had stolen the *ji'dar* swords, along with the diuturnal blades and all the other magical weapons that had gone missing over the past few months. What if they *weren't* behind the thefts, though? What if Matsumoto had been a victim himself?

It's been two months now, since the break-in.

Perhaps, he thought, some of his initial assumptions had been incorrect. He began going over the evidence—and, for the first time, questioning those assumptions that had led him to believe that the Dark was behind the thefts in the first place.

He started with the shadowy figure who had attacked him in the alley, after the Kite Labs robbery. The sneaker-wearing thief, who had made off with the *ji'dar* swords, had seemed to be Academy-trained...but that didn't necessarily mean he'd been *working* for the Dark; there were plenty of Academy-trained martial artists out there who no longer had anything to do with the syndicate. He might have been working for someone else, or for himself.

The Rhythm and his thugs could have been hired by someone else, too.

Did he have any real proof that the Dark had murdered Joe Arroyo? He had to admit that he didn't. It had certainly *looked* like their handiwork, and Sly had suggested that Rio had done the deed, but...

Maybe the Dark *hadn't* killed him. Someone had obviously wanted to silence Arroyo, but he was jumping to conclusions in assuming the syndicate was responsible.

His evidence was looking more and more *circumstantial* by the moment.

Ah, but what to make of Rio's appearance at the Nordic Heritage Museum, shortly after the place had been robbed? If his old enemy hadn't gone there to steal those Norse weapons, why *had* he gone there? What had he been doing, sneaking around the grounds in the middle of the...

Wait a minute.

Perhaps...perhaps, like Kaden, Rio had simply gone to the museum to *investigate* the theft. Perhaps he'd noticed the pattern as well—multiple thefts of unusual weapons—and had gone to the museum in hopes of catching the thief and recovering the stolen Satsujinken for his boss.

This was all speculation, of course, but Kaden couldn't find anything *implausible* in it. Maybe he'd been wrong this whole time; maybe the Dark *wasn't* behind the thefts.

But then...who was?

He had no idea. He had plenty of facts to work with, though—enough, perhaps, to build a whole new set of assumptions—and so, with a furrowed brow, he took it from the top once again, starting with the shadowy figure he'd encountered in the alley on the night of the Kite Labs robbery. Who had he fought that night? Who *was* the mysterious little ninja?

He didn't know...but it was obvious, from the way the thief had fought, that he'd been trained in the Dark's style. He'd either attended the Academy, or received training from someone who had.

There was something of the Dark's methods in Joe Arroyo's murder, as well. If the detective hadn't been killed by the syndicate, he'd been killed by someone who, at the very least, shared their slashy, murderous style. A disciple, perhaps? A former student?

The nature of the stolen items told him something, too. This thief, whoever he was, wasn't going after paintings, or jewelry, or bars of gold. He was collecting *weapons*—traditional weapons, like swords and knives. That suggested some kind of martial interest.

Maybe he was wrong about the syndicate being responsible for the thefts, or for Arroyo's murder, but *someone* with a connection to the Dark was mixed up in this case, he was sure of it.

The Academy had trained many, many students over the years, though, and that made the list of potential suspects rather long. Damon Rake, Jorgo, Talis Smoke...

He wondered if Sly might be able to help him narrow down that list. Sly's old friends, within the syndicate, might be able to...

He paused there, frowning again. Sly hadn't known anything about the thefts, and hadn't mentioned anything about the stolen Satsujinken. Were his contacts in the organization really telling him everything they knew?

Maybe, maybe not. Sly *had* been right about the attempt on Al Muranaka's life; he couldn't deny that. Rio *had* shown up to murder the reporter in his apartment, home-invasion style, just as Sly's contacts had predicted he would.

He found his thoughts drifting back to the night of the fight, and he scowled at the memories. It had been a desperate, fast-motion, close-quarters affair, a fight in a phone booth, and Rio had pushed and pressured him so relentlessly that he'd barely been able to...

And suddenly, all at once, he remembered something that, in his anger and frustration following the battle, he'd completely forgotten. He'd broken Rio's wrist that night—his right wrist.

And yet, just a few moments ago, he'd watched Rio pull open a door for Sho Matsumoto, using his right hand. He hadn't been wearing a cast, or a sling. His wrist hadn't appeared to be injured at all.

He couldn't have healed *that* quickly. Kaden had heard the carpal bones break. He'd *felt* them break.

What was going on here? What did this mean?

In searching for an explanation, his thoughts returned, once again, to the night of the fight...and the more he thought about it, the stranger the encounter began to seem to him. Rio, for instance, hadn't spoken a word throughout the fight, which was uncharacteristic, and the skills he'd demonstrated, especially towards the end of the battle, had been phenomenal. The man he'd fought in the apartment had been stronger, fiercer, more self-assured, and even more technically brilliant than the man he'd fought at the ballpark.

Had he even been fighting Rio?

What if...what if he'd been fighting someone *else?*

His fingers tightened around the steering wheel, until the knuckles turned white. There was only one man in Signal City who could've impersonated Rio like that; there was only one man who possessed that kind of martial skill with butterfly swords.

Of course. Of course. He felt like an idiot for not realizing it sooner.

It was Sly.

CHAPTER THIRTEEN

*I*t was ten minutes to midnight when Kaden arrived at the James J. Holden House, on the far northern tip of Stone's Row. The lonely old mansion, a Gothic masterpiece, had been built at the top of a high cliff overlooking the sea, about a mile from Signal City's most famous historical landmark: the Old Lighthouse. Built in 1939 by a wealthy steel magnate, the mansion had been partially destroyed by a fire during World War II, and lived in only sporadically after that. The crumbling, creepy ruin, nestled within a grove of skeletal trees and surrounded by an eight-foot-tall, wrought-iron fence, was rumored to be cursed.

Only a handful of people were aware of the *real* history behind the dilapidated mansion. That steel magnate, James J. Holden, had been one of the founders of F.A.N.G., a fifth-column terrorist outfit active from the 1940's to the early 1960's, and he'd built the mansion specifically to serve as a F.A.N.G. base: it was full of secret corridors, hidden radio rooms, and brutal-looking interrogation chambers. Moreover, the entire mansion had been constructed above an enormous, natural cavern, accessible to the sea, which F.A.N.G. had used as a covert submarine base during the war. The grotto's existence was still something of a secret, even after all these years, as was the hidden stairway in the mansion—carved out of the living rock—that led down into it.

About five years ago, the Dark, aware of the mansion's unique features, had considered moving the Matsumoto Academy there, and had sent Edge, Yeng, Sly, and a few others to inspect the place. Kaden and Rio had tagged along.

In the end, however, the Dark had decided not to bother with it, and it had remained abandoned. According to the information Kaden had just uncovered, it had changed hands several times since then; it was currently owned by a small real estate investment trust.

Confidence Realty.

Sly's "real estate" business was obviously a cover for whatever scheme he was running. On a hunch, Kaden had checked Confidence Realty's holdings, and the group's purchase of the Holden House had immediately jumped out at him. Sly, he felt certain, was using the place as some kind of hideout. Kaden didn't know what his old teacher was up to—or why, disguised as Rio, he'd tried to kill him at Al Muranaka's apartment—but he had every intention of finding out.

There didn't appear to be anyone home—there weren't any vehicles around, and the mansion's many, many windows (the ones that weren't boarded up, anyway) were all dark. Kaden, after studying the building for several minutes and seeing no signs of life, slipped through the fence, crossed the ruined garden, and climbed the crumbling concrete steps up to the terrace. The eastern door was locked, but the lock was old, and rusted, and he was able to bust it open without much effort.

Having been there before, he was more or less familiar with the mansion's layout. Entering through the eastern door had put him on the second floor, at the top of a landing; there was a large room—a picture gallery—to his right, and two smaller rooms to his left, at the end of a hallway. The main hall, nearly a hundred feet across, was below.

The building wasn't furnished. There were some shredded, ancient-looking curtains on the windows, and a few enormous wooden cabinets in the main hall, but for the most part the mansion was empty of furniture. Kaden turned on a flashlight and made his way down the grand staircase, to the main hall, looking for signs of recent activity. He didn't find any, but he knew better than to trust outward appearances here; there were dozens of hidden rooms in the mansion, and the grotto, far below, had its own set of facilities as well. It was possible Sly was using the grotto as a base of some kind.

The secret stairway, which led down into the cavern, was in the old library, a large room off the main hall. Kaden, shining his light into it, entered the room and looked around.

There wasn't much to see. The carpeting was rotten, the windows were boarded up, and the bookshelves, which had been built into the walls, were devoid of books; they'd been removed ages ago. A foul odor hung in the air; probably there were mice, or rats, living in the walls.

He looked up at the empty shelves. The long, winding staircase that led down into the grotto was behind one of these shelves—the middle shelf on the north side, he thought it was—but he couldn't remember the trick to opening it. He stepped back, contemplating the shelf, tapping the flashlight to his chin in an absent sort of way.

And then he heard a whisper in his ear: "Don't move."

Surprised, Kaden moved—he jumped, actually, and started to spin around, to get a look at the whisperer, but as he turned he caught sight of a long, silvery blade, glinting at his throat.

"Don't move," the voice repeated, "or I'll kill you right here." It was a feminine voice, rather monotone.

How the hell had she managed to sneak up on him? "Whatever you say," he grumbled.

She proceeded to disarm him, removing the tonfa from the sheaths on his thighs and the dart gun from his belt. Looking down, he noticed she was wearing sneakers. White sneakers.

"You're the thief," he said, as it dawned on him. "The one who attacked me in that alley and made off with those swords."

"Shut up. Hands behind your back."

He did as he was told. She tied his wrists together with a zip-tie, and when she was finished, said, "Now start walking."

"Where are we going?" he asked.

"Down."

She pressed a switch of some kind. One of the bookshelves fell back and slid aside, revealing a secret passageway. It wasn't the middle bookshelf, though, that slid aside; it was the larger one, just to the right, and instead of a staircase, Kaden found himself looking at a gigantic freight elevator.

This was new.

The girl, whoever she was, prodded him into the cage—that damn sword of hers was still on his neck—and pressed a green button. The elevator rumbled to life, lowering them down, down,

down, into the cavern; the deeper they went, the more Kaden began to smell the sea.

At last, the elevator came to a stop, and the gate swung open. The girl ordered him out, into the cavern.

It was even bigger than Kaden remembered it—at least a hundred yards, from one end to the other, and with a ceiling high enough to accommodate a three-story building. Several cinder block buildings had, in fact, been built in the cavern, along the water's edge, and several large chambers had been burrowed out of the walls as well, presumably by the original F.A.N.G. operatives. A concrete seawall had been constructed along the edge of the water, and a sort of iron scaffolding (from which several lights had been affixed) hung from the ceiling, suspended just a few feet below the stalactites. The mouth of the cave, which was only about fifteen feet across, was far away, to his right.

There was plenty of recent activity *here*. New generators, new pumps, new lights...and the squat, rust-stained cinder block buildings looked as though they'd been refurbished as well. He could hear voices coming from inside some of them.

"Nice," Kaden commented dryly.

The girl didn't respond to that. She turned him left, directing him into the deepest, darkest part of the cavern, where the F.A.N.G. terrorists had built their rock-walled chambers. Several of these chambers, he saw, had been converted into holding cells, with jail-cell doors, and she stopped him in front of one of these. She unlatched the door with another button press, prodded him inside, and locked the door behind him.

He tried to get a look at her face, as she walked away, but it was too dark; the lighting in this part of the cave was poor.

"Great," he muttered, pressing his forehead against the cold metal bars. "Just great."

"Don't feel bad," a voice said, from the shadows of the cell. "The little sneak got the drop on me, too."

Kaden turned around, squinting into the dark. "Rio?"

"Hiya, sweetheart. Happy to see me?"

"Not particularly." He followed the sound of his voice, into the dark recesses of the chamber. His eyes eventually adjusted enough for him to make out Rio's shape; he was sitting on a sort of crude bench that had been carved out of the rock. "How long have you been down here?"

"Couple hours, maybe. She put the cuffs on you, too?"

"Yeah. What's going on here, Rio? Who is she?"

"I don't know who she is," he said, shrugging. "I know who she's working for, though."

Kaden nodded unhappily. "Sly."

"Oh, so you figured it out, too?" He snorted. "Yeah. It's Sly. This whole thing is his operation."

"Do you know what he's planning?"

"I don't care what he's planning. He's a thief and a liar, and a traitor, too. I'm gonna kill him the first chance I get."

"He stole the Satsujinken from Matsumoto's collection, didn't he?"

"Yeah. And a bunch of other swords, from a bunch of other people. I would've figured it out sooner, but he's had me barking up the wrong tree for the past month—he told me *you* were the one who'd stolen the Satsujinken. He told me you had it out for the Dark."

"He talked to you?"

"Yeah, he showed up out of nowhere, just after the sword was stolen. Acted all friendly. Told me I was his favorite student." He spat.

"He told me the same thing," Kaden said. "And he warned *me* about *you*. He told me you wanted me dead."

"I *do* want you dead," Rio said cheerfully, "for the record. I've been busy, though, since I got back into town. Priorities, you understand."

"He was pitting us against each other," Kaden fumed. "He *wanted* us at each other's throats. He *knew* I'd be stupid enough to go after you; all he had to do was keep warning me not to."

"You two have *always* been easy to manipulate," a new voice said, from outside the cell.

It was Sly. Rio immediately rose to his feet and, pushing past Kaden, snarled at the man through the bars: "You smug bastard. You're gonna pay for this."

"Simmer down," Sly said. He turned on a nearby light, and Kaden realized then that the mastermind wasn't alone—there were two others with him. One was a beautiful, mature woman with long, thick black hair; the other was an adolescent girl, perhaps thirteen, but tall for her age, with blue eyes and long, blonde hair, which she had tied up in an efficient ponytail. She was wearing a ninja suit and a sword on her back.

White sneakers, too.

The thief. This was the girl who'd captured him and led him into the cell.

He knew her face; Izzy had showed him her picture.

"You're Olivia Pottinger," he whispered.

She turned to look at him, but her expression was blank, and she said nothing in reply.

"Yes," Sly said, glancing at the blonde girl. "Olivia Pottinger. And this lovely lady," he said, turning to the dark-haired woman, "is Alina Alkaeva. Hypnotika."

"Pleased to meet you," she said, eyeing them both in a predatory sort of way. She spoke with a thick Russian accent.

"Hypnotika?" Kaden had heard of this woman; Race had mentioned her several times. She was a metahuman, recently escaped from the Metahuman Correctional Center, who possessed an ability to hypnotize people with her voice. As he recalled, she'd been spotted in Stone's Row several times over the past few weeks.

A dark-haired woman with a funny accent? "Ah," he said. "So *you're* the one who's been going around abducting these kids." He glanced at Olivia, whose expression was still empty. "And you're brainwashing them, too. Lovely."

She merely smiled at that, and shrugged.

He turned to Sly. "I thought you'd gone straight."

"Nah."

"I thought we were friends, too."

He spread his hands; Kaden noticed he had a splint on his right wrist. "Sorry, kid. I'm a businessman, above all...and you know I'd never let a little thing like *friendship* get in the way of a good business opportunity."

"I'm gonna kill you, Sly," Rio growled. "Fair warning. I'm gonna kill you, and I'm gonna take back the Satsujinken."

He chuckled. "I think *she* might have something to say about that," he said, gesturing towards Olivia. "Show them, my dear."

Olivia reached behind her back and drew the sword out of the scabbard. It was a small, curved, silvery blade—a *kodachi*, with a blood-red hilt. The Satsujinken, the sword of death.

"You gave it to *her?*" Rio asked, bewildered. "What the hell for?"

"She earned it," he said simply. "Olivia here happens to be my best student."

"You're training these kids?"

"Well...sort of. It's more *programming* than *training*, in some ways; Hypnotika's been helping me insert some of the more advanced techniques directly into the students' minds. Really speeds things up." He gave the blonde girl a weird, fatherly look. "Olivia is special, though. She's speedy, and clever, and she has all the right instincts. I daresay she's better than either of you were, at that age."

"You kidnapped her."

"Yeah," he said lightly. "And you should've seen her that night at Doyle Station; she put up a hell of a fight. She actually managed to knock a whistler out of the air with the palm of her hand...and that was before she'd had any training at all! I considered releasing her, you know, after I discovered who she was, and after she started showing up on the news—I didn't like all that heat—but she was such a damn good recruit that I decided to keep her."

"You thought she was just another runaway kid that nobody would miss."

"Yeah." He chuckled. "I handed off the actual kidnappings to Alina after that, though. She's got more of a knack for it."

"I don't get it," Rio said. "Kidnapping kids, brainwashing them, giving them magical swords...what the hell are you *doing* here, Sly? Building your own private army?"

"Not exactly."

"It's not an army," Kaden said quietly, as the scope of his old teacher's plan became clear. "It's a new Matsumoto Academy. He's creating a rival syndicate."

"Something like that," Sly said, grinning. "There's a great need, in the underworld, for skilled bodyguards, spies, and assassins. For years, the students trained at the Matsumoto Academy were considered the best that money could buy...but *my* students are going to be even better. Absolutely loyal, perfectly obedient, programmed to fight and kill in a dozen different ways...and force-multiplied with unique weapons that will make them a match for most of the city's superheroes. I'm going to make a *lot* of money, hiring these kids out."

"They're just *kids*, Sly. The crime bosses aren't going to want to hire kids."

"They will when they see how effective they are...and of course, the older they get, the more effective they'll become."

"They're *kids*, Sly," Kaden repeated. "This whole thing is *sick*."

He waved that away. "I *had* to use kids, to start; kids are much easier to program than adults. Alina's influence over an adult will begin to fade after a few hours, if she's not around to maintain the spell. Kids are different; they're much more malleable."

"Zere minds are not yet fully formed," Hypnotika explained. "It eez possible to permanently rearrange child's psyche, if child is young enough."

The woman's voice, even apart from the accent, was very strange; it had a weird, silky-smooth quality to it, and it zoned him out for a second. Obviously this was her power at work.

Rio, still fuming, was unfazed. "I'm gonna kill you too, you witch," he snarled. "I'm gonna kill both of you."

Hypnotika glanced at Sly. "I do not like him."

Sly was apologetic. "He's always been a hothead. Good fighter, though, and *persistent*. Like a dog on a bone. When I found out Matsumoto had ordered him to find the Satsujinken...well, I knew I had to do something about it."

"You tried to get me to kill him," Kaden said.

"I tried to get you to kill each other," Sly corrected. "Both of you were closing in, from different sides. Rio was after the Satsujinken; *you* were trying to solve Arroyo's murder, and get to the bottom of that Kite Labs robbery." He frowned. "I made a mistake, hiring the Rhythm for that one. He's always been worthless. Fortunately I had the good sense to send Olivia along to keep an eye on him."

"You *did* kill Arroyo, then."

"Had to. He was getting close."

"You were afraid of the cops?"

"Of course not," he scoffed. "I just didn't want these kidnappings blowing up all over the news. I'm trying to keep a low profile here. So I killed him, and to cover my tracks I started playing the two of you against each other." He grinned. "It was pretty damn clever, you have to admit. I made *you* think Rio had killed Arroyo, and I told the hothead you'd stolen the Satsujinken, as a part of some crazy plan to bring down the Dark. I was hoping you'd kill each other, nice and clean, and save me the trouble, but Rio wasn't totally convinced, and *you* started putting things together more quickly than I expected. After you told me what you knew about the kidnappings, I decided I'd better just kill you quick and get it over with."

"So you set up an ambush, at Al Muranaka's place."

He nodded. "Muranaka's an old friend of mine. Very nice of him to let me use his apartment. *Unfortunately* I failed to finish you off." He shrugged. "But you know, that might have actually been a blessing in disguise. You're much more valuable to me alive than dead. Same goes for you, Rio."

"What are you talking about?" Rio asked, suspicious.

"I can use you. The two of you will make excellent operatives."

Kaden and Rio exchanged a glance. "You think we're gonna *join* you?"

"Well...not willingly, no."

Kaden's eyes turned to Hypnotika, who was still eyeing them in that predatory way.

Uh-oh.

"You're too old to be completely reprogrammed," Sly said. "But you can still be mind-controlled into following my orders. Isn't that right, Alina?"

"Oh, yes," Hypnotika purred.

"I can't believe you, Sly," Kaden said, shaking his head. "I can't believe you'd do this to us. After all the lessons, after all the years we spent together at the Academy..."

"We had some good times," he admitted. "I was actually thinking about bringing you boys on board at one point, as a matter of fact, but I knew you'd turn me down. Rio's too devoted to the Dark, and you, Kaden...*you* chose an entirely different path." He shrugged again. "It's funny how things work out."

"Life is full of surprises," Kaden agreed.

And *that* was the moment the White Ribbon appeared, exploding out of the water below in a sudden torpedo-blast of salt and spray. A single, ragged tendril, emerging from the midnight-blue of the water, quickly swept over the rocky ground, like a whip, knocking Sly, Hypnotika, and Olivia off their feet; Izzy then pulled herself over the seawall, dripping wet, and ripped the iron-barred door off its hinges with her ribbons, freeing Kaden and Rio.

Sly stared at the newly-arrived superhero in astonishment.

"Surprise," Kaden said.

CHAPTER FOURTEEN

"*T*ook you long enough," Kaden said, as Izzy sliced the plastic cuffs off him.

"You told me thirty minutes," she countered. "You all right?"

"Fine."

Rio, still cuffed, swept past them, racing away into the darkness. Hypnotika made a break for it as well, quickly climbing to her feet and heading for the freight elevator.

"We can't let her get away," Kaden told Izzy, raising his chin at Hypnotika's retreating form. "We need her to deprogram these kids. They've all been brainwashed."

"I'm on it," Izzy said, beginning to follow the fleeing woman. She was stopped in her tracks, though, by Olivia, who had kipped herself up and drawn the Satsujinken to bar her path.

She stared. "Olivia? Is that you?"

"Watch it!" Kaden shouted. "She's not herself!"

Izzy glanced at Kaden uncertainly, then turned her eyes back to the ninja-girl. "Drop the sword, Olivia. I don't want to hurt you."

She didn't budge.

Her eyes narrowed. "Fine." And one of her ribbons shot out, snaking its way towards the girl. She was fast, though, very fast, and the Satsujinken slashed out at the snake as it drew near.

Izzy's cloak immediately withered and shrank away from the blade, falling lifelessly to the ground. The entire cloak shuddered at the sword's touch, and at the same moment, Izzy shrieked and began clutching at her chest. She doubled over, falling to her knees.

Olivia closed in. Kaden immediately leapt to protect his fallen friend, scooping up a length of iron bar—a piece of the ruined door—and engaging the girl.

She turned to face him, slashing at him with the ancient sword. He was able to parry her blows, awkwardly, with the iron bar, but the bar was heavy, and a poor substitute for a real weapon. She quickly gained the upper hand.

Kaden was familiar with her fighting style, though, and he had a physical advantage besides—he was bigger and stronger than her, and nearly as fast. Finding the flaws in her form, he began using his strength to bull his way forward, driving her back, towards the edge of the water, all the while swinging the bar around like a club. Cornered, she tried to slip past him, but Kaden, anticipating this, managed to cut her off. Seizing her by the arm which held the Satsujinken, he whirled her around, picked her up, and flipped her into the water, some fifteen feet below. She was light as a feather.

Kaden rushed to Izzy's side. She'd stopped shrieking, but was gasping now, as though she were out of breath. "Are you all right? What happened?"

"I...don't...know," she wheezed. "Something happened...to the Ribbon." He helped her to her feet. "The magic in that sword..."

"I get it. Are you gonna be okay?"

"I think so. Only..." She screwed her face up in concentration. "There's something wrong. The Ribbon feels...numb. I can't get it to move."

Kaden studied the cloak, which was looking very ordinary at the moment. "That's a problem."

But it wasn't the only problem. While Kaden had been battling Olivia, Sly had jumped to his feet and sounded an alarm. Half a dozen kids, dressed in black, ninja-style outfits, and all armed with swords, sais, *kama*, and other weapons, suddenly emerged from the brick buildings and, at Sly's urging, charged Kaden and Izzy.

"I'll hold them off," Kaden said urgently. "*You* go after Hypnotika."

"But—"

"We *can't* let her get away."

"But without the Ribbon, I don't think I can—"

"Forget about the Ribbon. *You're* gonna have to run the red light tonight, Izzy."

She took a deep breath. "Okay," she said, nodding smartly. And she ran for the freight elevator, her cloak flying behind her.

Kaden, grimacing, tightened his grip on the iron bar, fell into a defensive crouch, and waited for the charging children to attack.

This wasn't going to be easy. True, these kids were only kids, but they were trained (or programmed, anyway) to fight, and all were armed with magical weapons. One was holding a shortsword, glowing bright red; another was cracking a long, fiery bullwhip; and a third—a pretty brown-eyed girl, about eleven or twelve—was wielding a golden staff. He had no idea what these weapons might be capable of.

And he was going to have to fight these kids, and disarm them, without seriously injuring them.

It wasn't going to be easy at *all*.

The first thing he needed to do was rid himself of the iron bar, and get his hands on a real weapon. The brown-eyed girl, with the staff, was the first to reach him, so he went for hers: after parrying a couple of her strikes with the bar, he dodged a big downward smash and kicked her backside as her momentum carried her forward; knocked off-balance, she fell to the ground, and on her way down he snatched the golden staff out of her hands. Discarding the bar, he then blocked the red-glowing blade with the staff, just in time, and parried a series of blows from another kid wielding a gray-steel sword —probably one of Epee's diuturnal blades. The blows shuddered the staff, sending tremors up Kaden's arms.

By then the kid with the flaming whip had jumped into the fray. He cracked it in Kaden's direction, filling the air with yellow sparks and forcing him to retreat.

Kaden paused, trying to figure out how to fight the kid with the whip. He couldn't get close to him, with all the other kids in the way, and he didn't have anything to throw at the little whip-master, either, to keep him at a distance. *Damn.*

The whip cracked again, blasting him with heat. He ducked it.

Meanwhile, the other kids were continuing their assault, coming at him from all sides. He used the staff to knock the legs out from under the kid with the glowing shortsword, took a moment to parry a pair of sai-thrusts, then jumped back and went around-the-world with the staff, spinning it helicopter-style over his head, forcing the kids to back off a bit.

None of these kids were the equal of Olivia—fortunately—but he was still badly outnumbered here, and he still didn't know what to do about the kid with the whip, which weapon was once again cracking just over his head. He wished he had more time to think; the other kids were closing in again, forcing him to keep fighting.

An older boy, probably about thirteen, jumped to the front of the line, attempting to stab him with a forked spear. The tip of this spear, which he only narrowly avoided, was crackling blue with electricity; Kaden caught it under his arm, slapped the kid across the face with the golden staff (he hated to do it, but it was his only option under the circumstances) and wrestled the weapon away from him. Now, with the staff in one hand and the spear in the other, he pushed his little attackers out of his way and took a chance, charging the kid with the whip.

The whip-kid held his ground. Drawing his arm back, he gave the flaming flail another crack. To protect himself, Kaden raised the spear, and the whip wrapped around it. The kid quickly yanked the spear out of his hand...but that drawing-back of the whip gave Kaden a split-second opportunity, allowing him to rush forward and slap it out of the kid's hand before he could bring it to bear again. Yelping in pain, the kid tried to retrieve the infernal thing, but Kaden kicked it into the water, where it sizzled into steam and disappeared from sight.

He had no time to rest on his laurels, however; the other kids had already regrouped. A pair of swords came flashing towards him, a *kama* bounced off his breastplate (without the armor, it might have plunged into his chest), and the kid with the sais returned to stab at him. Kaden defended himself as best he could, but, unwilling to strike back at the mind-controlled kids, and finding more of them popping up all the time, was slowly but surely driven back.

He couldn't win this one. He had to make a break for it.

Unfortunately the fight had carried him *away* from the freight elevator, and at least seven ninja-kids now stood between him and that exit. Even more worrisome, the kids had begun to coordinate their actions; they were spreading out, trying to flank him.

He needed to get out of the grotto. He couldn't make it to the elevator, and the mouth of the cave, which opened up to the sea, was far away; swimming for it was out of the question. Was there another way out?

He suddenly remembered the long and winding stairway—the original connection between the mansion and the grotto. Had Sly sealed it off, when he installed the elevator? Scanning the area, he spotted the tunnel, leading out of the main chamber, where the stairway had been excavated—it was nearby, fortunately—and started fighting his way over to it. This was a gamble; if Sly *had* sealed it off, he could easily find himself cornered in that tunnel.

Dodging swords and shurikens, Kaden made it into the passage, and was relieved to discover that the stairway was still there. All the while blocking, riposting, and turning aside the swords of his attackers, he entered the gloomy, stone-carved stairwell, and began to work his way backwards up the steps, while fending off the kids coming at him from below. He had an advantage here; there wasn't enough room in the dark, narrow stairwell for Sly's brainwashed minions to gang up on him. They had to fight him one-on-one here.

He was getting tired, though; the kids were wearing him down. He was sweating under his body armor, and beginning to breathe hard.

Still, he fought on—dodging, ducking, thrusting, and kicking at his attackers, just to keep them at bay. About halfway up, he landed a lucky strike that knocked a bigger kid off his feet and sent him tumbling down the stairs, bowling over the smaller kids behind him. The nimble ones hopped over the tangle of bodies and continued after Kaden, but the pile-up took a bit of the pressure off.

A red-headed kid with a yellow dagger jumped at him; Kaden batted him away. The brown-eyed girl, now recovered (and anxious to retrieve her staff), came at him with bare fists, trying to force her way into his space; he stamped her foot with the butt of the staff and pushed her back into the mob.

It took every trick and technique he'd learned at the Academy to make it up those stairs, but, at last—and just as he was beginning to wonder if this stairway-battle would ever end—he managed it. At the top of the stairs, he quickly pulled the lever that slid the big bookcase aside and slipped through the gap, into the library, just ahead of the kids' blades; then, seizing the bookcase with both hands, he muscled it shut again and jammed a handy piece of detritus into the mechanism, sealing the kids in the stairwell.

He stopped for a moment to catch his breath, leaning heavily on the staff. Close call.

He was just considering how he might go about disabling the freight elevator as well when he suddenly heard the sounds of a struggle coming from the mansion's main hall. Rushing into the dark, haunted room, he looked up, and saw Izzy battling Hypnotika on the second floor; the two of them were fighting over a stiletto, at the top of the grand staircase. Izzy, he was relieved to see, had apparently regained some measure of control over her magical cloak—she'd managed to wrap a single ribbon of cloth around Hypnotika's mouth, to prevent her from speaking.

She needed his help. Raising the golden staff, he started for the stairs...

...But was stopped in his tracks by Sly, who suddenly burst forth out of the gloom, slashing at him with a devilish-looking katana.

"I don't think so," Sly grunted.

Kaden, surprised, parried the blows with the staff, but it was a furious assault; the sword was a silver whirlwind in Sly's hands. Finally, deflecting the blade with a baseball swing, he jumped back a few steps, and the two of them circled each other warily.

"Not bad," Sly commented, as though they were back at the Academy, and this was merely another training session. "You've come a long way, kid."

"I had a good teacher." It was hard to believe it had come to this —fighting for his life against one of his oldest friends, a man he'd long considered a sort of surrogate father.

"I know you did. I'm sorry about this, Kaden. I wish things could've been different."

"Don't patronize me, Sly." He snorted at his old teacher. "You don't give a damn about me. You never did. You're just like all the others at the Academy."

Sly smiled in a sad, mysterious sort of way. "You're wrong about that."

And he resumed his attack, the katana slashing horizontal. Kaden blocked that strike, and the next, but found himself unable to counterattack—Sly was coming at him so quickly, and with such skill and precision, that he simply couldn't find any openings. Worse, he seemed to be able to read Kaden's mind, snuffing out every one of his sequences before it could even begin. The same thing had happened during their fight at Al Muranaka's apartment.

How was he supposed to defeat the man? Sly had *taught* him how to fight; he knew every technique, every counter, that Kaden might call upon. The fact that Sly was fighting one-handed was something that he *thought* he might able to exploit, at first, but his teacher seemed to have a whole array of one-handed styles at his disposal, and he couldn't figure out how to get past them.

Sensing his frustration—and increasing desperation—Sly paused for a moment to gloat. "Give it up, kid. It's hopeless. I know everything you know, and then some."

"Didn't I break your wrist a few days ago?"

"You got lucky. Besides, you were using your tonfa then; you're more dangerous with tonfa. I've got a *sword*, Kaden. You're not gonna beat me with a *stick*."

And *that* was when the inspiration struck. Sly was right; he couldn't beat the man using the skills he'd learned at the Academy. Sly knew how to counter the Academy style.

Kaden's training hadn't ended at the Academy, though. It just so happened that, in the years since he'd left the Dark, he'd also picked up a few things about fighting with a staff.

Resolved, he changed his stance, bending his knees slightly and switching to the modified Yin-and-Yang grip that Quentin preferred.

Sly raised an eyebrow. "Oho? What's this?"

"Come see for yourself."

Shrugging, Sly swept towards him, his sword a cyclone fury. Kaden focused on the blade and batted it away as it came near— once, twice. Quentin tended to add a great deal of theatrical flowers and flourishes to his movements, to distract his opponents, so Kaden did likewise, slapping Sly's katana aside with the spinning staff and counterattacking from odd, unpredictable angles. This kind of improvisation was dangerous—Sly very nearly slashed his arm off at one point—but it was *effective*; the sword-master seemed to have no answer for it. Before long, Kaden was pressing *him* back, driving him all the way across the main hall.

"Cute," Sly said, scowling.

Kaden, growing more confident by the moment, continued his assault—juking, feinting, and spinning the golden staff into Sly's space. He fell into a sort of rhythm, and a curious, almost tranquil feeling began to creep over him. The staff became an extension of his body, as he whirled it all about the mansion's moonlit hall, and time itself seemed to slow down. Sly's blade snaked out, again and again, but Kaden, perfectly calm, caught it each time and turned it aside. He didn't know if there was some kind of magic in the golden staff, or if he'd simply tapped into some kind of inner strength, but at that moment, he felt invincible, untouchable.

"Damn," Sly said, genuinely surprised. "That's some pretty impressive–"

But he never finished, because Kaden, still swept up in the flow of battle, suddenly saw a perfect opportunity to strike. Pummeling the man, left, right, left, he stepped inside his guard, pivoted around him, and struck him across the side of the head with the end of the staff. This was Quentin's signature move, the one Kaden had never been able to get right; somehow, in this strange, Zen-like state, he'd finally managed to pull it off.

The cracking blow knocked Sly out instantly; the sword fell from his hands, and he collapsed to the floor. Kaden, out of breath, and struck by how suddenly the fight had ended, held his position for several heartbeats, the staff seeming to vibrate in his hands.

One blow.

He'd done it. He'd beaten him.

It took several *more* heartbeats for the Zen-like feeling to fade. Belatedly remembering Izzy and Hypnotika, who were still fighting over the stiletto on the second floor landing, he spun the staff back into an overhand grip and ran for the stairs.

He was stopped a second time, however, by the sound of machinery—grinding gears—which he heard coming from the library.

The elevator.

He'd forgotten about the still-functioning freight elevator. While he had been fighting Sly, the brainwashed kids—unable to break through the jam at the top of the stairs—had returned to the grotto and taken the elevator up to the mansion; now, they came pouring out of the library, a dozen of them at least, all armed with those diabolical weapons. They quickly surrounded him.

He grimaced. He didn't have the energy to fight these kids off a second time, and they had him dead to rights now, anyway, in the center of the main hall. He wasn't seeing a way out of this one.

Kaden was a fighter, though, if nothing else, and he intended to go down swinging. Wearily, he raised the staff...

"Tell them to back off," he heard Izzy say, in a low voice.

He turned his gaze up the stairs. Izzy, having gained control of the stiletto, was holding the blade to Hypnotika's throat.

"Tell them to back off," she said again. "And no funny business. If I start feeling for a second like you're trying to hypnotize me, you're gonna bleed."

The dark-haired woman, her teeth bared in anger, reluctantly complied. "You vill put your veapons down, *rebyata*," she said to the kids, in that bizarre, silky-smooth voice of hers. "You do not need zem right now. You are not feeling like fighting, yes? You do not vant to fight; you are very peaceful, yes?"

The kids set their weapons down.

Relieved, Kaden lowered his staff and sighed deeply. "I'm really getting to like you, you know," he told Izzy.

She smiled. "I know."

* * *

They herded the now-compliant kids back into the elevator and locked them up in the old F.A.N.G. holding cells, along with a dazed Sly and a bound-and-gagged Hypnotika.

"I'm not really thrilled about locking them up," Izzy said unhappily. "The kids, I mean."

"I don't think we have a choice. They're dangerous."

"What's going to happen to them? Do you think they can be...deprogrammed?"

"I don't know. If we can't get Hypnotika to do it, we'll have to consult with a psychic—Lester Cross, maybe, or that guy Darby Fray out in Boston. I hear he's pretty good at sorting people out."

"So now what? We call the police?"

"Actually, I was thinking of getting the Eyeball out here. Hypnotika's already escaped from the cops a couple times before, and Sly's damn tricky. We'll need to be extra careful getting them into custody." He threw her a sideways glance. "How's the Ribbon?"

"Still feels numb," she said. "But I think it's getting better. What about you? You're not hurt, are you?"

"I'm hurt all over," he said. "But I'll be okay. I think I might have..."

He trailed off there. He thought he'd heard something, over the sound of the water lapping against the seawall.

"What is it?" Izzy asked.

"I'm not sure..."

And then, all at once, a dark, lithe figure came sprinting out of the darkness, ninja-quick, and with the Satsujinken poised to strike.

Olivia! How could he have forgotten Olivia?

It all happened in a split-second. Izzy was closest to her, and it was Izzy she attempted to stab, racing up to her at all speed, charging at her with the cursed sword as though it were a spear. In vain, Izzy tried to call upon the Ribbon to protect her, but the cloak, shuddering, failed to respond.

Kaden, though, a mere two steps away, *did* respond. He responded without thinking.

He leapt in front of her, shielding her with his body.

Olivia's blade, full of speed, pierced him just below the ribcage on his left side, sliding in almost all the way to its blood-red hilt.

He gasped at the shock, and the pain, and the horror. The sword, lodged in his gut, was incredibly cold; he felt as though he'd just been stabbed with an icicle. He turned his head, and found Izzy's eyes; they were wide with terror.

Olivia, still grasping the hilt, promptly jerked the blade out of him. A fountain of blood followed it out, and he immediately crumpled to his knees.

"Damn," he muttered. "Oh, damn." It was strange; though Olivia had pulled it out, he could still feel the chill of her blade within him.

Olivia, for her part, was unmoved; her face was as blank and expressionless as ever. Flinging Kaden's blood off the Satsujinken—it splattered all over the cavern's rocky floor—she raised the sword a second time, preparing to strike down Izzy.

Kaden tried to rise, to stop her, to take this second blow for Izzy as well, but with his lifeblood leaking out, he simply didn't have the strength. Feebly, he reached out for Olivia, trying to grab at her. She ignored him, her full attention now on Izzy.

No!

Izzy backed away, but not fast enough. The Satsujinken darted out...

...And was slapped away by another sword, streaking out of the half-light. From out of nowhere, a tall, shadowed figure had suddenly burst onto the scene, right in front of Olivia, and begun driving her back, pummeling her with strikes and slashes. Clashing steel rang through the air.

Kaden stared. Rio. It was Rio.

Surprised by his sudden appearance—where the hell had he *come* from, anyway?—Olivia faltered and gave ground. Pressing his advantage, Rio hammered away at her, relentless, using his greater height and reach to bear down on her. To her credit, the girl hung in there for several seconds, but Rio's jarring blows were simply too much for someone of her size. Realizing she was outmatched, she feigned a counterattack, turned, and tried to make a break for it, but Rio stopped her—grabbing her by the scruff of her neck, he spun her around and knocked her out with a single, brutal punch to the face. She went down hard, her sword clattering to the stone.

Rio gave the girl a contemptuous snort. "Keep practicing, kid." He bent down and picked up the Satsujinken. "I'll be taking this," he said. And then he approached Kaden.

Izzy, now desperately trying to stop his bleeding, made a move to block him, but Rio leveled the sword at her. "Don't," he warned. And reluctantly, she backed down.

Kaden glared up at his old friend. "Rio..."

"This reminds me of something," he said softly, the tip of his sword hovering near Kaden's throat. "You remember that night on the rooftop?"

"I...remember," he managed.

"You could've killed me then." He studied him silently for a long moment, his expression strange and contemplative. Finally, to Kaden's surprise, he lowered the sword and shook his head. "Nah."

"Rio...I..."

"We're not friends, Kaden. We'll never be friends again. But this...this makes us even." He glanced at Izzy. "He's probably gonna die," he said matter-of-factly.

"No," she said fiercely. "No, he's not."

Rio chuckled at that. Sliding the Satsujinken into its scabbard, he stepped away, and strode off towards the elevator. He paused, though, at Sly's cell.

"You'll never see it coming," he told the man, his voice full of menace. And with that, he left.

Izzy returned her attention to Kaden. "You're *not* gonna die," she said, her eyes full of tears.

"Not...so sure about that," he said, struggling to speak. He was growing very sleepy, and the cold that had entered his body with the sword seemed to be spreading to his limbs. He couldn't feel them anymore.

"No," she said, determined. "I won't *let* you die." And then, more to herself than to Kaden, she whispered, "I'll save you. I'm a hero, damn it."

He smiled at the words. Izzy's soft, reassuring voice, speaking quietly to him over the lapping of the waves, was the last thing he heard before the darkness settled in and swallowed him up.

CHAPTER FIFTEEN

*H*e awoke in a strange place: a dim, windowless room, nearly
empty, with polished, dark-oak walls and a grand, crackling fireplace
in one corner. He was lying in an enormous, antique four-poster bed,
with red silk curtains and soft, velvety pillows. A heavy woolen
blanket had been draped over him, all the way up to his chin, but
despite this, and despite the fire, he still felt cold.

He wasn't alone. A lovely, dark-skinned woman, with long,
braided black hair, was sitting in a chair next to the bed, whispering
something under her breath. Her eyes were closed in concentration,
and her hands were moving as though they were caressing an
invisible ball. She seemed to be sitting in a column of faint white
light, but—and this was the damndest thing—he couldn't make out
where the light was coming from.

The woman looked vaguely familiar, but Kaden, groggy, and still
waking up, couldn't quite place her. Who was she? Some kind of
angel?

Was he dead? Was he dreaming?

The woman opened her eyes then; they were a dark, chocolate
color. "Good morning," she said kindly, in a lightly accented voice.
The strange, enveloping light faded away.

"Who...where...?"

"Excuse me," she said, rising. "I told Quarterstaff I'd let him
know the moment you woke up. He's been rather worried about

you."

Quarterstaff? Quentin? Kaden, full of questions but too tired to reply, could only watch as she exited the room, through a giant, iron-hinged door.

She returned a few minutes later, by which time he'd shaken off the worst of the grogginess. Quentin was with her; he was masked, and in costume. He gave Kaden one of his big, toothy grins.

"How ya feelin', kiddo?"

"C-cold," he said, his teeth chattering.

"That will pass," the woman said. Kaden recognized her now; she was Enchantryn, the superhero-sorceress who was second-in-command of the Paranormals. "Another blanket might help, though. I'll go find one." She left, closing the door behind her.

"Quentin...where are we?"

"The Alcott Library," he replied, "in Stone's Row. This is the Paranormals' headquarters."

"How did I get here? What's going on?"

He sat down on the bed. "Kind of a long story. What's the last thing you remember?"

Kaden frowned. "I...I was in the grotto beneath the Holden House, with Izzy. I'd just been stabbed."

"Yeah. That was a week ago."

"A week? A whole week?"

"You were in pretty bad shape. No real organ damage, fortunately, but the sword nicked a major artery. They had you in surgery for almost five hours. You're *very* lucky to be alive, kid."

"Surgery? How...how did...?"

"Miss Rushforth. She got you out of that cave and took you to Wyman Memorial in Wellington. *Very* resourceful young lady." He looked amused. "Anyway, the surgeons fixed you up. Good, clean job, as these things go."

"What did she tell them? Did they suspect...?"

"That they were treating a vigilante?" He chuckled. "Almost certainly. They won't talk, though, if that's what you're worried about; I've already seen to that. I happen to be on Wyman's board of directors."

"I see." He looked around the room. "None of that really explains what we're doing *here*, though."

"Ah. Well, you see, though the surgery was a success, your

overall condition failed to improve. The doctors couldn't wake you, for one thing. They were totally baffled. What they didn't know was that the wound wasn't merely physical; there was a *spiritual* dimension to it as well."

"Oh. You mean...?"

He nodded. "They don't call it the 'sword of death' for nothing. The Satsujinken cut into your spirit as well as your body. Eventually, Izzy figured out what was going on and contacted the Paranormals. They moved you here, and Enchantryn's been working on you ever since, putting you back together again." He gave Kaden a little slap on the knee. "You owe her *big*. You should probably send her some flowers or something."

"Yeah."

"Anyway, it's sounding to me like she expects you to make a full recovery. Another few days and you'll be good as new." He gave Kaden a rare serious look. "You really had me worried for a while there, kid. I don't know what I'd do without you."

Kaden smiled. "Thanks, Quentin. I hope you didn't fly all the way back here on my account, though."

"Nah. I got the call from Izzy on the flight home. Not sure how she got my number–"

"You talked to Izzy? Where is she, anyway?"

He shrugged. "In school, I imagine. It's Friday morning. She's been coming to visit you in the afternoons. I should probably send her a text, actually, to let her know you're awake. Before I do that, though..." He frowned. "I got most of it from Izzy, but I'd like to hear it from you. How the hell did you get into this mess, kid?"

Kaden took a deep breath and told him the entire story, from beginning to end. Quentin listened quietly, his only reaction being a scowl whenever Sly's name was mentioned. "I had a little conversation with him a few days ago," he said. "Didn't like him."

"Where is he now?"

"Locked up in the MCC."

"The Metahuman Correctional Center? Why? Sly's not a metahuman."

"It's for his own safety."

"Oh. The Dark?"

"Yeah. They're *very* unhappy with him, from what I understand. It's probably only a matter of time before they catch up with him."

"What about Hypnotika? What about the kids?"

"They've got Hypnotika in the MCC, too. There's been some talk about sending her back to Russia; she's been wanted over there for a long time. And the kids are fine, for the most part. Lester Cross has been working with them, rebuilding their psyches and erasing their memories of the past few months. A few of them will probably need some additional therapy—I've set aside a little money for that—but I think they'll come out of this okay in the end."

"Olivia?"

"Already back home with her folks. She's one tough cookie."

"And the magical weapons?"

"Back where they belong. We handed the *really* dangerous ones over to the Paranormals for safekeeping."

He sank back into his pillow. "All's well that ends well, huh?"

"Well, not entirely. Rio *did* get away with the Satsujinken."

Kaden shook his head in dismissal. "I'm not too worried about that. Matsumoto will probably just throw it in a closet or something; the sword was never anything more than a collectible to him."

"And Rio?"

He shrugged. "We're even, now. That's what he told me. I don't doubt we'll meet again someday...but for now, I think I'll take your advice for once, and stay out of his way."

"Let the dead Past bury its dead," he agreed. "I know this has been tough on you, kid, but you did good, very good. Maybe you could've avoided being *stabbed*–"

"I was defending Izzy."

"Yeah, she mentioned that." He grinned, in a wolfish way. "She really cares about you, you know."

"I...I like her, too," Kaden mumbled.

Quentin gave him a wink and an elbow. "You sly dog."

"Shut up."

"She's got real potential as a superhero, too," he opined. "That cloak of hers can do some pretty amazing things." He scratched his chin. "She *could* use some more experience, though. I wonder if she'd be willing to spend a few months working with us."

"With...us?"

"Do you think she'd be interested?"

"I don't know. She *does* have a bit of an independent streak."

"Well, it couldn't hurt to ask. We need all the help we can get out there." His face grew troubled. "You know, I've been thinking, kid—it's possible I've been pushing you too hard lately. If you ever start to feel like this life isn't for you..." He left that hanging.

"It's okay, Quentin."

"Are you sure?"

He nodded. "I've been giving it some thought, too, actually."

"Oh?"

"I may have gotten into this business for the wrong reasons," he admitted. "More because I like to fight than because I'm desperate to do good. But lately...lately I've been finding *new* reasons, *better* reasons, to stay in the game."

"Izzy?"

"Well...partly, yeah."

The masked man smiled and clapped him on the shoulder. "All right. I'll take your word for it." He stood. "You'd better get some rest."

"Thanks, Quentin. For everything."

"No problem."

He started making his way over to the door. "Oh," he said, stopping suddenly. "I keep forgetting." He fished something out of his pocket and tossed it to him. "Here you go. I think you've earned it."

Kaden caught the object in the air and examined it. He laughed softly.

It was a Snickers bar.

* * *

He was up and about the next day, and well enough to go home the day after that. Izzy, on a weekend vacation with her parents, was unable to see him until Monday—his first day back at school.

Race found him at his locker that morning. "Hey! Kaden! How're you feeling?"

"Still a little sore," he confessed. "Getting better, though."

"It must've been a pretty gnarly crash."

"Yeah. Good thing I was wearing a helmet." Quentin had put it out that he'd been in a motorcycle accident. "You got my homework?"

"Yep. You've got a lot of catching up to do, I'm afraid. Hey, did you hear the latest? The Big Leaguer tried to break into the SCPD's Special Armory last night. It was all over the news. Brazen and Shortstop showed up to stop him; I think they said Girl Friday was in there, too. There were lasers going off all over the place! I'll have to show you the footage at lunch."

"Looking forward to it," he said.

"Oh, and Hypnotika's been captured, too. Apparently she kidnapped a bunch of kids, and was trying to turn them into her own personal army or something. They found her right here in Stone's Row! That's pretty close to home, huh?"

"Yeah." He gave Race a sidelong look. "Did they say who captured her?"

He nodded. "New hero. She's called the White Ribbon. Nifty name, huh? I haven't seen any pictures or videos of her yet, but the buzz is she's pretty impressive. She'd have to be, wouldn't she, to capture Hypnotika?"

"I suppose so," he said, amused.

"Do you think she's based here in Stone's Row?" He grinned a huge grin. "Man, that would be cool, wouldn't it? We might actually start seeing her flying around town, live and in person!"

"That *would* be cool," he agreed.

Russell appeared a moment later. "Good to see you, man," he said, slapping him on the back. "You all right? I heard about the crash."

"Yeah, I'll be okay."

"What about the bike?"

"Totaled, unfortunately."

"What kind was it?"

"Ninja ZX-14. 2016."

"Ah, that's a shame. That's a nice bike."

Kaden raised an eyebrow. "You're into bikes?"

"My old man's a collector," he said. "He's got over a hundred of 'em in the showroom, including some really old ones. He's got a 1907 Harley, and a Winchester...and a 1915 Cyclone Board Track Racer, too, in absolutely *pristine* condition."

"A Cyclone? Really?"

"Yeah. Paid over a million for it. You'll have to come over and check it out sometime."

Kaden gave him an appreciative nod. "Thanks. Maybe I will."

The two of them, Russell and Race, headed off to class then, leaving Kaden cracking a little smile at his locker. Maybe he didn't *need* any friends, here at Jeffries, but he was glad to have them.

He loaded the locker up with the stack of homework Race had given him, closed the door...and found himself eye-to-eye with Izzy.

"Hi," she said, a little uncertainly.

"Hi," he replied. "Are you free? Let's go somewhere and talk."

They made their way up to the old storeroom on the second floor. They'd had their first real conversation in this same room only a few weeks back, but to Kaden it felt like a lifetime ago.

"You're looking good," Izzy offered, after they'd closed the door behind them. "I mean, you're looking *healthy*. Does it still hurt?"

"A little. Enchantryn put a couple of spells on me to deaden the pain, though, and speed my recovery. Only catch is I can't eat meat for the next three days." He shook his head. "Don't ask me why. Magic is strange stuff."

"Tell me about it." She chewed on her lower lip for a moment, then said, "I was really worried about you. I was sure you were going to die."

"I would have," he said evenly, "if not for you."

"You saved *my* life before I saved yours," she pointed out, "when you jumped in front of Olivia's sword. We're even, if anything."

"I don't know about *that*. How is Olivia? Have you seen her?"

She nodded happily. "She's fine. Or she *seems* to be, anyway. Her parents were thrilled to have her back."

"Well, that's all thanks to you. You stuck it out; you didn't give up."

"I couldn't have done it without you." She hesitated. "You've...you've really helped me, and not just on this kidnapping case. I've been wanting to tell you this for days now: I finally let my parents know that I wanted to be a veterinarian."

"Oh? How'd they take it?"

"They weren't happy," she admitted. "My mother, especially. There was a lot of yelling. But I *did* get through to them, in the end. They said they'll let me train for it...on the condition that I get a degree in biology first, at my Dad's old school."

Kaden grinned. "That's great news."

"Yeah. And...I have you to thank for it."

"Me?"

"*You're* the one who insisted it was my decision to make—all that stuff you said about running the red lights. And when you jumped in front of that sword, and almost died in my arms..." She spread her hands. "How could I be afraid of my mother, after going through all that? Maybe this sounds weird, but...when you took that sword for me, you gave me some kind of courage." She smiled. "I guess that's what heroes do, right? They give people courage."

He frowned.

"What's the matter?"

"Nothing. It's just...it still feels wrong, being called a hero."

She stared. "How can you say that? You risked your *life* for me, Kaden. You took the stabbing that was meant for me. That's called *self-sacrifice*. What could possibly be more heroic?"

He shook his head. "I don't think it counts."

"Why not?"

"Because it wasn't just anyone I was protecting. It was you." He took a step forward. "At this point, I think I'd do just about anything for *you*."

She blinked. "Oh."

"I know you've been having doubts," he went on, "about whether you're really meant to be a superhero. It's something I've been struggling with, too." He held a hand out to her. "I'm sure of one thing, though: I want to be with you. Maybe...maybe we could try looking for answers together."

She looked up at him, with her pale blue eyes. "Sounds good to me," she said quietly, taking his hand.

He pulled her into his arms. "I'm gonna kiss you now," he warned.

"That...that sounds good to me, too," she said, smiling shyly.

Kaden smiled back.

It was a very, very long kiss.

ABOUT THE AUTHOR

Blake Michael Nelson was born and raised in a rural part of western Minnesota. He's been writing fiction since he was eight years old.

Made in United States
Orlando, FL
04 December 2023

39937639R00085